*The Last Year of the Season*

# The Last Year
## OF THE
# Season

John Michael McLaughlin

NORTH STAR PRESS OF ST. CLOUD, INC.
St. Cloud, Minnesota

For Julie

Cover art by: Reva Graves, socialbug.com

Printed in the United States of America

Published by
North Star Press of St. Cloud, Inc
PO Box 451
St. Cloud, MN 56302
www.northstarpress.com

Chapter 1

# Thursday of the First Week of Football Season

SEPTEMBER IN ST. LUKE OFFERED the most spectacular sunsets. For miles in every direction, harvest was underway, and dust in this driest of months rose behind combines like smoke from Cain's offering, trapped between heaven and earth. A blend of dirt, crop dust, and diesel exhaust filtered the glow of the sun into the warmest colors of the spectrum while azure blue hovered overhead. Assistant Coach David Anderson stood motionless at the ten-yard line, once more awestruck by the beauty of the sky over his hometown.

"It's a timing play for crapsake. It's a timing play. Five steps out, and three steps over, and the ball will be in your gut. We'll do it again and again until that puke-pink sunset fades away and until Coach Anderson makes sure every one of his receivers can count to eight without using their fingers." It was vintage Carl Tucker. Head Coach Carl Tucker had run that play and demanded perfection from his players even before David had played for the Lettermen. Coach Tucker despised losing, and this hatred had built St. Luke into a Minnesota football dynasty.

Forty-five minutes later, as David turned to head to the locker room, Carl groused and put his right hand on David's good shoulder, "This is my twenty-fifth year as head coach, David. For crapsake, I think I'm ready to hang it up."

"Carl, you've been saying this for years," David interrupted.

"No, it's different this time. This is a good team, but we haven't been tested. If we beat Elk River in two weeks, we're for real. I want to go out a winner. I have no worries about you taking over as head coach. You're ready whether it's next year or the year after."

"We've got a dominating team every year, Carl."

"But the stars are aligning: twenty-five years as head coach of the Lettermen, a team that might just take it all the way, and the Rule of 85. I started with St. Luke thirty years ago, 'fresh out of North Dakota State,'" David said in unison with his mentor with a combination of humor and irritation.

Carl looked at David with a quizzical expression, then picked up the story. "Right, now I'm fifty-five. Thirty plus fifty-five equals eighty-five. I can stop now and use the average of my last three years of earnings as my retirement base, and, bingo, I'll fish and hunt while Bobbie makes her eighty-five; then we're done. Being remembered as a winner is all I want."

David had never taken it seriously that Carl and his wife, Bobbie, the district's chair of the special education department and head of the teachers' association, would retire—at least not in their mid-fifties. He felt sure the talk he'd heard time and again was just that—talk—and when the reality of retirement approached, the Tuckers would put it off in favor of their dedication to the public schools of St. Luke, Minnesota. But today Carl's tone and the look in his eyes were different. Instead of the casual indifference with which he usually responded to Carl's retirement dreams, David swallowed hard. "Let's get by Elk River before you make an announcement," he said.

While David knew he would take the head coaching position when Carl retired, he was in no hurry. Following Carl Tucker would be an immense challenge, the high school equivalent of following Bear Bryant at Alabama. David loved coaching, perhaps as much as Carl, but David's fondness for the classroom far exceeded that of his mentor. David had broken the tradition of football coaches teaching social studies and was a popular teacher of English. Being head coach would relieve him of two of his classes, leaving him with a half day of teaching and a full day of coaching.

He hadn't expected to enjoy teaching literature as much as he did. Coaching was his first desire, but teaching English was his access point. Yet over his years of classroom preparations, constant reading, and countless discussions of art and literature with his wife, David had grown more and more passionate about his teaching. He loved his American literature course, where he emphasized the historical backdrops of the greatest books of the nation. He used the incongruity of being a six-foot-three football coach who appreciated books to reach and motivate students who regarded literature as feminine, time-consuming, or irrelevant. He dearly loved teaching the fall semester elective he had created—Minnesota Writers—focusing on authors like Sinclair Lewis, Jon Hassler, Garrison Keillor, and Kathleen Norris. It made Minnesota the land of the living word. In spring he followed with Communication for the Twenty-First Century, always filled and usually limited to seniors. The head coaching position would end these courses.

Getting choked up was uncharacteristic of David. He was strong, confident, energetic, and committed. He was used to standing on solid ground, on a firm foundation, sure of his next move. At Carl Tucker's certainty, David felt a tremor in that foundation. His life was intimately intertwined with the two most powerful men in St. Luke. Carl's retirement would cause a shift in the balance of David's life. He knew there would be much to discuss tonight with his wife, Katy.

\* \* \*

THE DRIVEWAY TO KATY'S CHILDHOOD home was the longest in town. The home, built by Katy's great-grandfather, expanded by her grandfather, and remodeled by her father, Victor Gram, was by far the grandest in St. Luke. However, the driveway was the real show of wealth. Most houses in Katy's hometown had short driveways to lessen the snow shoveling. This home's long driveway was a public display that other people shoveled the Grams' drive. The driveway gracefully curved for a hundred yards before it forked to either the back of the house with an attached four-car garage beneath the rarely used guest accommodations or to the grand circle at the front entrance where valets would park cars when Katy's father entertained. Tonight, Katy pulled around to the back and didn't even notice the car parked at the front.

Katy was picking up her eighteen-month-old daughter, Anna, later than planned. Her father was home already and Harriet, Victor's cook and housekeeper, was watching Anna. Katy had just finished a planning session for a field trip to Normandy, Brittany, and Paris. Though she no longer taught French at the high school, Katy was excited to help plan and chaperone the French class trip. She had taught the current seniors during their tenth-grade year before she took maternity leave to have Anna.

Harriet and Anna greeted Katy in the kitchen. "How's my little sweetheart?" Katy cooed as she hugged Anna. "Mommy wasn't gone very long, was she?" Anna, nestled in her mother's arms, sucked her thumb. "It smells wonderful in here, what's Dad having for supper?"

"Chicken cordon bleu, wild rice, and blueberry muffins," Harriet replied as she stirred a simmering pot. "You know how he loves those muffins."

"You spoil him, Harriet," Katy chided.

"That's what he pays me to do," Harriet said. "Besides, he's a pleasure to cook for, always thankful, always a gentleman. He's a good deal more appreciative than your grandfather, who got pickier and pickier in his later years."

"Where is he? We've got to go kiss Grandpa, don't we, Anna?"

"In the library with a guest, a mister so-and-so from Cleveland or California or somewhere far away. He's not from around here. I let him in about a half hour ago."

As Katy approached the library, she could hear her father's voice. "Gram Industries manufactures a wide array of specialized printing inks, our main line being newspaper inks. To remain competitive, I need a better educated workforce. The complexities of production and environmental compliance require reading and thinking skills that simply weren't necessary twenty years ago. Our high school, where most of my employees come from, isn't keeping up. In fact, it's putting out an increasingly weaker product."

Katy popped her head through the doorway. "Excuse me, Dad, may Anna and I say hello and goodnight?" Victor rose and kissed Katy on the cheek.

"Of course. Always family before business. Anna, did you enjoy helping Harriet fix my supper? I'm sure you were a big help," Victor boasted as Anna climbed into her grandfather's arms.

"We'll get going. I've got to get supper for David. I just wanted to let you know the meeting was very productive. Plans are coming together, and we may even expand the trip to include the south of France. Now I'm going to run—"

"Wait a minute," Victor said as he nuzzled Anna's cheek, "let me introduce you to someone." Katy was stunned. She was used to meeting her father's guests and business contacts, but this was no middle-aged acquaintance. Harriet was right. This man was definitely not from St. Luke.

"Katy, this is Jack Taylor. Jack, my daughter Katy and granddaughter Anna. I met Jack through a mutual friend in Chicago. Jack is founder and CEO of a company called Aclare Learning, based in San Francisco. He has a product he thinks can improve the performance of the high school."

"*Bonsoir*," Jack greeted her. "*C'est un plaisir de vous rencontrer. Est-ce que je vous ai entendu dire que vous allez à Provence? J'ai une maison et un petit vignoble juste en dehors de la ville.*"

Katy managed a, "*Oui.*" *Oh, my,* thought Katy, *great-looking and speaks perfect French. Where did Dad say he met this guy?* In perfect rhythm, Katy responded, "*C'est exact, j'accompagne les élèves de terminale lors de leur voyage en France.*"

Still holding her hand, Taylor offered, "*Vous pourriez peut-être loger chez moi. Vous avez combine d'élèves?*"

*I wish he would let go of my hand. We're beginning to melt together,* Katy thought.

As Katy and Jack spoke, a palpable energy flowed between them. Victor watched, hugged his granddaughter, and shook his head almost imperceptibly.

\* \* \*

WITH ANNA TUCKED IN, David and Katy stood at the sink. He washed, she dried. The window blinds were open over the sink.

5

Through the darkness, David enjoyed the sense of peace offered by the lights in their neighbors' homes: Rick and Jennifer Slade with two-year-old James, Anna's playmate; Jim and Joan Robertson, both in their eighties and the original owners of the home built in 1949; and Brooks Myers, a professor at St. Cloud State University, who had recently lost his wife to ALS.

Katy and David had made a handsome home together. With David's carpentry skills and Katy's eye for color, they had turned a run-down, late-1940s-era house into a beautiful home. David loved working on the house. While his friends lived for outdoor activities like golf, fishing, and hunting, David was a homebody. Being with Katy and Anna was his joy. Having them near as he refinished a banister rail, set tile in the bathroom, or installed a new light fixture was a treasure.

Katy had always loved color, and decorating came easy to her. To her amazement, however, she had a wonderful sense of space and could visualize a change in their home far ahead of David. Katy could create. David could execute. Together they had opened up the main floor of their house by taking out the non-load-bearing walls. The effect was dramatic. It created a greater sense of family. Katy and David hadn't set out to build a dream home. Instead, they had focused on a place to raise children even before they had Anna.

In the window over the sink, David could see the reflection of Anna's toys strewn across the front room floor. He could see his desk and Katy's desk next to one another in the corner, and the bookshelves filled with his beloved American literature. He could see several awards he had won for his teaching as well as the openings where he was replacing two rails on the banister. He could see Katy drying a pot, and he could see himself. He appreciated the comfort he and Katy had created, but he was restless. Something was bubbling just beneath the surface. He hoped Katy would draw it out, not by speaking, but by listening with the ear of her heart.

As pleased as David was with their home, he knew he had paid a steep price for it, not the real estate loan he and Katy had assumed in their second year of marriage, but the price of pride. When Victor Gram learned they had bought the house on Cherry Lane, he was beside himself. "You bought an old rental house in the Morningside neighborhood?" he'd asked in disbelief. David would not soon forget the walkthrough they arranged for Victor before the closing. The realtor had let Katy, David, and Victor into the empty house, then left them alone. Victor walked at a slow but steady pace, hands behind his back, footsteps echoing off the wooden floors as he took in every facet of the house: rough and stained floors, tacking strips that used to hold carpeting, cracks in every plaster wall and ceiling, light fixtures with frayed wiring, two abused bathrooms, and a kitchen that could only be described as disgusting.

Katy had wanted to show her father the house after she and David had spent a few months fixing it up while they still lived in their apartment. She knew what her father's response would be and what issues it would trigger. David expected his father-in-law would be upset, but he wanted Victor to see the house in its worst condition, not to create a scene, not to question if that was the best two young public school teachers could do, but to benchmark the condition of the house so that Victor would later appreciate David's skills as a craftsman and his devotion to making a home with Katy.

"Katherine, David, please let me help." Victor had contained his shock at the condition of the house. "I can't stop you from buying this house, but let the wealth from three generations of Grams fix it up for you. I don't want Katherine Gram scraping off wallpaper, sweating like a worker at my factory, cleaning other people's dirt. Katherine, you deserve the best," Victor declared.

"Dad, I have the best," Katy responded, placing her arm around David.

David was surprised Victor's reaction had been so restrained. Victor was still cautious with his daughter and her husband of eighteen months. Pride was an issue for David, pride mixed with insecurity. For as much as he had accomplished before his twenty-first birthday, he had reason to be proud. But pride for those accomplishments was not his sin. Rather it was the pride in not letting Victor help, in insisting that he and Katy make it on their own, in denying Victor the pleasure of helping, in placing Katy in a position to have to refuse her father.

David couldn't remember the first time he had seen Katy. He knew when he was a child that Victor Gram had a daughter. The Grams were the first family of St. Luke, and the entire town was saddened by the cancer of Victor's wife, Anna, and mourned her death. David remembered thinking, when he learned that Anna Gram had died, that he didn't even know Katy Gram, but they had something in common; they had both lost their mothers.

David had seen little Katy Gram at town functions and Gram Industry picnics, but he had been a boy then. Katy had seen David when, on breaks from boarding school, she had attended the Lettermen's home games, but David was little more than a cute jock. Their lives didn't truly intersect until David had played his last football game and Katy had seen the world.

\* \* \*

DAVID BECAME COACH CARL TUCKER'S greatest accomplishment, quarterbacking the Lettermen to undefeated seasons and state championships in his last two years of high school. David was a national blue-chip college prospect. Six schools in the Big Ten, Notre Dame, Auburn, and USC recruited him most heavily. Minnesota was where his heart lay, but the Gopher program was in transition, lacked stability in the coaching staff, and played in the antiseptic Metrodome. He chose Iowa on account of Hayden Fry and Kinnick Stadium and because he would have an opportunity, if things went well, to be the starting quarterback his sophomore year.

And things did go well. David became Iowa football. He held the starting quarterback role for almost three full years, three glorious years in the reign of King Hayden. David was royalty at Kinnick, yet among the thirty-thousand students in Iowa City, he was able to walk almost in anonymity. He enjoyed the campus and took every opportunity to soak in the cultural life—theater, music, and art exhibits. This puzzled David. It was incongruous with his upbringing.

He knew he wanted to coach high school football after a pro career, and that would require a teaching major. By the close of his second year, he declared his major, English Education. Jon Densford, an associate professor who focused on the early writers of the prairie, agreed to be his adviser. David was amazed that a Southerner from Memphis would have such affection for the northern plains. In Densford, David found an inspiring academic adviser.

Seamlessly, David mixed his reading, critiques, and character analyses with his football life. He read constantly on buses and planes, while being taped, shaved, iced, and massaged, at the training table, in his dorm room, and on Friday nights before games. Literature was a gigantic jigsaw puzzle, and each great work he read added another piece. He knew he would never see the puzzle fully completed. It would never be complete, but he longed to see as much of it as he could. Unexpectedly, David's reading hours would increase dramatically.

It was October of David's senior year, early in the third quarter of the game with the University of Indiana. The Hawkeyes had things well in hand, 24 to 7, and were driving for another score. If the Hawkeyes added seven more points, David would take one snap on the possession after the touchdown, then trot off the field to a standing ovation as his substitute entered the game. David was being discussed as a Heisman Trophy contender. Michigan was coming to Kinnick Stadium next week, and Fry would want his star rested and healthy to take revenge for the Hawks' only loss the previous season.

With third and seven at the Indiana forty-five, Fry called a short drop pass where David would roll right. The Hawkeye offensive line had handled Indiana's pass rush easily through the first half, but Indiana's All-American linebacker, Patrick DeKnight, had broken through the Iowa line three times. David knew a blitz was likely from Indiana. As he was

9

under center, he checked DeKnight's location. The linebacker was just off to the left, which would give David an extra step as he rolled right to throw. On the snap, David stepped back and rolled right. His receiver was perfectly positioned. Just as David was about to release the ball, DeKnight smothered him. David was driven to the turf with his arm extended over his head, dislocating his shoulder and breaking his humerus.

It was a hit David had taken before, but this time the angle, mass, and velocity combined to spell disaster. The game was delayed fifteen minutes as a silent Kinnick watched David in agony on the grass. A gurney rolled across the field, and Iowa's football idol was lifted onto it and loaded in an ambulance. Excruciating pain numbed David's mind. He had no thoughts that his playing days were over, that in one brief moment his income for the next academic year would go from $1.6 million to $30,400. He didn't know that his father would still have to work for a living. He didn't suspect that teaching would ultimately be his primary income, not his post-NFL pastime.

David watched the remainder of the season from his hospital bed. His injury had been even more severe than the initial field diagnosis. There had also been a separation of the shoulder and fractures in the rib cage just under his right arm. He was in surgery for four hours at the University of Iowa Medical Center, the first of three surgeries and eight months of rehabilitation that would restore David's right arm to health but not to fortune.

The Sunday after the Indiana game, a pilgrimage started to David's room. Hayden Fry and the Iowa coaches and trainers were in early, then teammates, at first as many as the hospital would allow and then a steady stream of ones and twos. They found David sitting in his adjustable bed, looking like he was hailing a cab, right arm extended with the forearm at a 120-degree angle. Surrounding his shoulder was a plastic cuff that restricted his movement, and from his bicep to his bluish-purple fingertips was a plaster cast supported above and below by the traction system.

By the second week, the media attention evaporated, and the

interest of the coaching staff faded. His football career was over. He was yesterday's hero. His true friends from the team and campus continued to visit, but David slumped towards depression. DeKnight's tackle had forever changed his life, yet David wasn't angry at him. Although the hit had been ferocious, it had been clean. David knew he was lucky to have had such a successful football career. It was more than most could ever dream of. He also knew careers and lives could change on a dime with slips on ice or dives in pools. But, like so many athletically graced young men in America with the promise of a professional sports career, David had no Plan B, at least not one he recognized as he mended in the hospital.

David was reading Rolvaag's *Giants in the Earth* when there was a knock on the door. "Come in," he said in an uncertain tone. The medical staff and his friends just came in without knocking, so who could be calling on him?

"Excuse me. Have I come at a bad time?"

A combination of bewilderment, excitement, and embarrassment washed over him as a beautiful woman with a warm smile stepped into his room. Who was this? There was something vaguely familiar about her, but he was sure he had never met her. He was suddenly self-conscious. He had been in the hospital ten days, and despite his and the hospital staff's efforts, he looked far from his best. Since no shirt sleeve could be pulled over his right arm, he had worn nothing but hospital gowns with the right sleeve unattached for ten days. "No, please come in. I just wasn't expecting anyone."

"I can come back later, when you're . . ."

There was a pregnant pause, which David eased with a grinning, "Asleep?" The remark was just silly enough to break the ice.

"I'm Katy, Professor Densford's research assistant," she said as she shook David's left hand.

"Densford came by a couple of days ago. I think he wanted to make sure I wasn't slacking off on his reading list." David laughed, holding Rolvaag in his hand. "Are you a fan of the prairie writers?"

"No, I work with Densford on translations of French explorers. He doesn't read French, at least not very well. You're an English major?"

"Well, a secondary teaching major with an English emphasis. I was pleased Professor Densford agreed to take me as an advisee. He's about the only prof I've got who doesn't make a big deal out of my being a football player. As a matter of fact, until I got hurt, I wasn't even sure he knew I play . . . uh . . . played for the Hawks. I like that about him. Are you a grad student in English?"

"Not exactly. I grabbed the R.A. role with Densford because I speak and read French . . . at least better than he does. I'm in the master's program in French education."

"Say something in French for me."

Katy blushed, hesitated, then said "*J'ai pris plaisir à te regarder pendant ces années*. Do you speak French?"

"No," David said, with the beauty of her words echoing in his ears.

"Good," Katy puffed. "Then I haven't embarrassed myself too badly."

"So why did Densford send you over here?"

"He didn't exactly send me. I volunteered."

"What do you mean?"

"I didn't realize he was your adviser until he mentioned you yesterday and said he needed to get some reading assignments to you. I told him I'd take them to you, that it might be nice for you to see someone from your hometown."

David shook his head in confusion.

"I'm Katy Gram."

"Katy Gram!" David said. "*The* Katy Gram, Victor's daughter?"

"One and the same."

"You're one of the few people from St. Luke I don't know."

"I used to watch you play for the Lettermen when I was home from school. I feel like I know you. You've got quite the public persona on campus, and you did back at St. Luke too."

"Public persona?"

"Yes. People talk about you so much, and you're so written about that strangers think they know you."

"How come we've never met before?"

"I guess it just wasn't time."

Katy was easy to talk with. David was able to be himself more with her than with any other girl he had known. He was forever thankful he'd had two minutes of conversation with her before he learned her last name. It had made all the difference. If he had known who she was before she came into his room, it would have been different—stilted, uncomfortable.

\* \* \*

THE MONDAY AFTER THE HAWKEYES lost to Minnesota, David was released from the hospital. The traction apparatus had been adjusted little by little until, on discharge, his right arm was immobilized against his abdomen. It felt wonderful to be out of the hospital and able to walk the campus again. As anxious as David was for his release, there was a nagging thought in the back of his mind. Over the past two weeks, his most frequent visitor had been Katy Gram. As a messenger from Professor Densford, Katy fulfilled her mission. David was kept abreast not only of Densford's class but his other classes as well. Apparently, the professor had reached out to all of David's teachers and coordinated, through Katy, his studies.

Katy's visits from the very start had been about more than academics. He learned about her life as the daughter of St. Luke's first family. He learned about her life away from St. Luke: boarding school, the Ivy League, summers abroad, places he had never heard of, activities he'd never dreamed about. He learned about her love of the French language, art, and wine. Through conversation in a sterile hospital room, without even holding his hand, Katy won his heart. Whether she had intended that result or whether the feeling was reciprocated, David didn't know, and the loss of the hospital room as their meeting place was unsettling.

His uncertainty was short-lived. Waiting for him on his return to his dorm room was a letter from Katy, inviting him to her apartment the coming Sunday to watch the presentation of the Heisman Trophy. David was ecstatic. As he sat on her sofa watching an event that should have had him center stage, he said, "I never thought I'd win, but I did hope I'd be there." That admission unleashed the first display of emotion since his injury, a single tear down his left cheek. The tear's path was stopped by the lips of Katy Gram, a kiss responded to with an embrace by a left arm, which resulted in two sobbing people whose hearts were laced forever.

\* \* \*

As KATY DRIED THE SILVERWARE, David leaned back against the sink. "Carl says he's retiring at the end of this year."

"Carl's been retiring for years."

"I know, but this time he seems serious. The stars are aligning—a state championship's in sight, the Rule of 85, and numerous Elvis sightings in the area. Oh, I don't know. I just feel he's going to do it this time."

"So even if he does, we've known he'd step aside at some point and you'd take over. That's something you've looked forward to, not Carl retiring, but your being a head coach. Right?" Katy said.

"I think so, but now that it's here, I wonder." David pulled his wife close to him and whispered in her ear slowly, "I like teaching better than coaching. Being head coach will cut out half my classes. I'd hate that."

Chapter 2

# *Monday of the Second Week of Football Season*

Monday nights from mid-August to early November held a well-established routine for the Andersons and the Tuckers. David, Katy, and Anna would arrive at Carl and Bobbie's at six thirty. After a quick hello, Carl and David would go to the boathouse, while Katy and Bobbie enjoyed wine and prepared dinner.

Carl's boathouse was a total man's getaway. Calling it a boathouse was an understatement. It was a cabin with a full living room, bathroom, and small kitchen. It also had a spot for Carl's boat and a concrete drive to the lake, which allowed Carl to winch his boat directly out of the water and into a spacious, heated garage. Just outside the boathouse, Carl had a thirty-foot dock off of which he regularly sank bales of straw and other materials ideal for nesting panfish. When the fish were biting, Carl and David would watch tapes of their upcoming opposition through the open double doorway, playing and re-playing the tapes with the remote control, on the dock fishing the entire time.

David had learned more fine points of the game from watching tapes with Carl than he had during his four years at Iowa. Carl sized up every member of the opposition like a stockman considering which head to buy at an auction. He reviewed each player, checked the number on his jersey, evaluated his height and weight, approximated his speed, and considered how the Lettermen matched up. Carl studied the plays—the sequence, frequency, and characteristics of what the coaches called in critical situations. He kept his thoughts in a spiral notebook, one notebook for each year he had coached. These notebooks were a history of his coaching career, filled with data about his teams and their opponents as well as day-to-day reminders of grocery lists, retirement funds, and an occasional personal reflection. Carl nimbly referenced them. While all the players transitioned through high school, the coaches remained fairly stable. As the old man of the league, Carl knew his opposing coaches' strategies often better than they knew them themselves.

Carl breathed football, and on Monday nights David sat at the foot of the master. Until ten o'clock, interrupted only by supper, they would watch, fast forward, rewind, slow-mo, cross reference Carl's notebooks, and outsmart the opposition even before the lights came on in the stadium.

There was another purpose to Monday nights as well—Bobbie, Katy, and Anna. As soon as David and Carl retired to the boathouse to watch tapes, Bobbie and Katy talked about everything under the sun. Katy had been twelve when she lost her mother. Bobbie was childless and a full generation older. Bobbie was deeply caring, highly intelligent, and lovingly maternal. Everything she did, she did well. Everything she cared about, she studied. And everyone she loved, she loved without reservation. And she loved the Andersons. If there was ever a doubt that the Tuckers and the Andersons would be lifelong friends, the deal was sealed with Anna. Anna was Bobbie's surrogate granddaughter. Bobbie kept up with every aspect of Anna and had albums full of photos with every major event and milestone. Katy knew that if anything ever happened to David and her, Anna would live with Carl and Bobbie. It was in their will, and despite her father's deep objection, Katy knew Anna would be loved on a full-time basis at the Tuckers', not raised by hired help and loved by Victor after business hours.

This Monday Bobbie served grilled pork tenderloin marinated in Italian dressing. While Carl and David drank beer, Bobbie and Katy enjoyed a glass of wine. Bobbie made a skillet of cornbread and squash and beans from her garden. The table had an arrangement of asters and mums and looked over a glassy Lake Arrow, which abutted the Tuckers' manicured lawn. It was a scene made for *Midwest Living*.

"So, Katy, how is the planning going for the spring trip to France?" Bobbie asked, sipping her wine.

"Very nicely, thank you. And, David, I forgot to tell you that we may add Provence to the itinerary!"

"Terrific. How did that happen?" David mumbled through his first bite of cornbread.

"Well, it came about after the meeting last week, which, by the way, went very well. The students are dedicated to doing every aspect of the trip right. Planning, budgeting, and scheduling—the whole works. They're a great group of kids. Anyway, after the meeting, I went to pick up Anna from Dad's, and he had a business associate with him who overheard Dad ask me about the planning meeting, and, *voila*, he steps up speaking flawless French and offers us his small villa outside Toulon. Knowing Dad's friends, I'm certain this won't be a small villa. I haven't talked to the planning group about it yet, but I'm sure we'll take it. It fits our schedule, expands our tour, and it won't cost anything."

Katy looked at David, who was reaching for another piece of cornbread. He seemed just fine. The flawless French had not annoyed him. David felt her look and smiled. He knew what she was after and asked, "Say, who is this generous Francophile?"

"Let's see, he's definitely not from around here. He's a Californian, I think, and his name's simple. Let's see, Joe, John, no, Jack. That's it. Jack, Jack Taylor."

"Not *the* Jack Taylor, I hope" Bobbie said in a joking tone.

"Who's *the* Jack Taylor?" inquired David.

"Why was this Jack Taylor visiting your father?" Bobbie asked.

"Dad said they had met through a mutual friend in Chicago."

"Who is *the* Jack Taylor?" David asked again.

"Well, if Katy's met *the* Jack Taylor, she'll never forget him. He's devilishly good-looking, polished as brass, can charm anyone out of their socks, and he's public enemy number one for public schools across the country."

"What? Who? I've never heard of this guy," Carl grumbled. "Ever heard of him, David?"

"Nope, but what makes him public enemy number one?" David asked as he put down his fork to listen. Carl followed suit as Bobbie wiped her hands with her napkin.

"I first heard about Jack Taylor at the association's national convention in July. He's one of a handful of Wall Street rich guys who thinks he can improve public schools. His company's made a mess of a number of schools on the East Coast. There was a story on him in this month's newsletter from the state association. I've thrown it away, but the title was something like, 'If It Sounds Too Good to Be True.' Katy, is this the man who was at your father's house?"

"I don't know. He certainly fits the good-looking description, but I was so startled when he spoke French I don't remember what Dad said he did or what company he was with. And why would *the* Jack Taylor come to St. Luke?"

David, seeming a bit distant, noted, "He must have been doing some business with your father. St. Luke's schools are great. There's no need for his company here."

"You can say that again," added Carl. "We're one of the best school districts in Minnesota, and Minnesota's one of the best education states in the country, so that speaks for itself. I'd say we're in some rarified air. Let's get back to dinner. We've got film to watch."

"All the same, I'm curious," Bobbie persisted. "If this was *the* Jack Taylor and if he was visiting your father on business, it's still worthy of note. Maybe I'll call St. Paul. The union might know something."

"Enough, enough, enough. We've got film to watch. Bobbie, would you please serve dessert? It's football that keeps St. Luke on the map, and a loss this Friday to that bunch of eggheads from St. Cloud Tech would be nothing but an embarrassment. Come on, David, grab your plate."

It was almost eleven o'clock when David and Katy drove home, with Anna asleep in her car seat. "Wow, I'm still stuffed. Bobbie's pork tenderloin was divine, and I've got leftovers so we don't have to cook!"

David didn't respond. "So, are you ready for the game? You boys left the table pretty early, especially to prepare for a cream puff like St. Cloud Tech."

"Yeah," David said with an uncharacteristically flat tone. "Look, look, thanks for trying to draw me out. I know I'm irrational on this point, and I was just fine until you confirmed that Jack Taylor was devilishly good looking, but . . . the French thing," David laughed, "I'm goofy on this."

"You betcha, baby."

"I love you with my whole heart and trust you without reservation, but your French is still very special to me and, well, you know the rest."

Katy placed a kiss on David's cheek and whispered, "I could not ask for a more honest man. You are goofy, but you're getting better. Let's get home so I can speak some more French to you. *L' honnêteté a ses récompenses,*" she said as David smiled.

Katy held David's hand as she leaned her head against the window and watched the lights and street signs go by. A light drizzle was falling, just enough to create a glow around the street lights. As Katy read the street signs of her hometown, she felt sleepy and relaxed, cozy and warm with her husband and daughter. Halfway home she popped up and shouted, "Clare Way! That's it!"

"What?" David asked. "We don't live on Clare Way."

"No, no," Katy stammered. "Clare, clare something. That's it, Aclare Learning. That was *the* Jack Taylor I met at Dad's. Aclare Learning's the name of his company!"

"That's interesting, but that doesn't mean he was here about St. Luke's schools. Wait a minute. Were they talking about schools?"

"Yes, yes, they were. As I was walking down the hall to the library, I heard Dad complaining that the St. Luke graduates he hires aren't good enough, lack critical skills. You know what Dad's always saying."

"Yeah, he wants rocket scientists from the bottom quartile of the senior class."

"Yeah, and Dad said Jack Taylor may be able to offer some help to the high school."

"Great, maybe Taylor will replace my Minnesota Writers class with Reading Poorly Written Manuals for Asian-Made Electronics. Why didn't you remember this at the Tuckers?"

"I don't know. You know what being a parent has done to my short-term recall. It was the street sign, Clare Way, that jogged my memory."

"You going to call Bobbie when we get home?"

"Yeah . . . well, I don't know. That's Dad's business, and I can't betray his confidence. All through my childhood I'd hear Gram Industry plans—expansions, promotions, legal stuff. We never spoke about it outside the family."

"But Bobbie needs to know."

"I know. But I can't be the one to tell her, and neither can you. If Jack Taylor has St. Luke in his sights, she'll know soon enough. But, still, I hate not being able to tell her."

Chapter 3

# Wednesday of the Second Week of Football Season

I<small>T DIDN'T TAKE LONG FOR</small> S<small>T</small>. L<small>UKE</small> to learn that Jack Taylor had been in town. On Tuesday, Bobbie had been intensely busy. She taught her morning classes and spent the afternoon as usual in her office. She was on a special assignment for the district, her role to assure that the rights of students with handicaps were upheld under the Individuals with Disabilities Education Act. As the district prepared for a federal audit of the last three school years, hundreds of files had to be reviewed to assure that all the mandatory processes and notifications had been respected and all the required signatures were obtained. It was a tedious but critical responsibility.

Wednesday proved to be a bit easier. Right after lunch she called Bruce Barnes, head of the state teachers' association. Bruce said he wasn't aware of Jack Taylor being in St. Luke but he'd nose around a bit and see what he could find out. At three o'clock, he called back.

"Good work, Bobbie. You're right. Jack Taylor *was* in St. Luke. How'd you sniff out that fuckin' scumbag?"

Bobbie recoiled from the receiver. "Well, St. Luke is a small town. What I want to know is, how did you confirm it so quickly?"

"We think these Wall Street bastards are a real threat, and national has dedicated some resources to following them, understanding their networks, and, usually, knowing their whereabouts."

"Sounds kind of cloak and dagger for a teachers' association."

"There's an awful lot at stake here, Bobbie. Say, how'd you know he was up there? Did you see him? Did he meet with some school board members? If so, maybe we can catch him early on a sunshine violation."

"No, I didn't see him, and I don't know whom he met with. I just heard he was here from a reliable source."

"Well, we know Taylor's no fisherman, it's not hunting season for a few more weeks, and he's got no family up that way. That doesn't mean he wasn't here on other business, but St. Luke's a small district compared to the big cities where his Aclare Learning has been screwing things up. It doesn't make sense to me."

"Me neither, Bruce. I appreciate your information."

"You're welcome. Let me know if anything develops in St. Luke."

Bobbie hung up with a heavy heart. She stared at the phone for a moment, then picked it back up to call Katy. "Katy, I put you in an awkward position Monday night regarding Jack Taylor. I'm sorry. I didn't mean to ask you to break your father's trust."

"Bobbie, don't worry. I wasn't playing dumb. I didn't put the pieces together until we were driving home and passed Clare Way. Then the lightbulb came on. I've wanted to talk with you ever since."

"Well, I learned from St. Paul this afternoon that Jack Taylor was here. Bruce Barnes doesn't know why Taylor visited St. Luke or whom he met with, but he's suspicious."

"Thank you for not letting Bruce know that Taylor met with Dad, but after Friday's *Leader* comes out, it will all be public."

"What do you mean?"

"Dad called me last night. He knows a guy like Taylor can't just slip in and out of St. Luke without being spotted. But, get a load of this, Jack Taylor got picked up for speeding just outside town on Highway 10 after he left Dad's. It'll be in Friday's paper. So Dad had breakfast this morning with Superintendent Keegan and has asked that Aclare Learning be on the school board agenda in two weeks."

"Goodness, let me catch my breath. So Taylor *is* targeting St. Luke, he's making an auspicious introduction to the community by being listed in our weekly paper's Traffic Log, and your dad has already met with Ken Keegan to put Aclare on the board agenda."

"Well, you know my father. He's used to getting things done, and he's used to getting his way. He also met with Sam Tolofson of the *Leader* and with one of his staff writers to explain why he's asking the district to consider Aclare. It's a proactive strike to get public opinion behind him early."

"Will that be in tomorrow's paper?"

"I should hope so. I can't imagine Tolofson wouldn't scramble to get the story into this week's edition. By next Friday the whole town will be talking about Aclare, and the *Leader* will live up to its tagline, 'If It Happens in St. Luke, It's News to Us.'"

Bobbie chuckled and then was silent. "Thanks, Katy," she finally said. "Maybe Aclare will kick up a lot of dust and never gain a toehold. Well, I've got to perform my duty as local teachers' association head."

"I know. Don't worry about me. Between the Tuckers and Victor, I'm covered in St. Luke. I just hope Aclare doesn't change things."

"It won't. This isn't the right place for Aclare."

"Is there a right place for Aclare?"

"I don't know, but I know it's not here."

\* \* \*

THE ARTICLE IN THE *ST. LUKE LEADER* set the town abuzz. Aclare was the topic at restaurants, barber shops, beauty parlors, and dinner tables. Victor may have wanted to get his opinion out early, but it was a good thing the Lettermen were on the road, whipping St. Cloud Tech 42 to 0 that Friday night. If it had been a home game, more than likely members of some vocal subgroup, strengthened by a few Grain Belts, might have encouraged one another to drive by the Gram mansion and shout their opinions on Victor's plan.

As it was, hundreds of conversations about Aclare took place in twos and threes, among family and friends. While opinion varied from outrage against to outright support for Aclare, the overwhelming majority were puzzled by Victor's desire to improve the high school. The people of

St. Luke could safely read of educational disaster areas, dismal test scores, record-breaking dropout rates, and school shootings and rest comfortably in their prairie isolation, assured that their school district was the crown jewel of the community. Bad schools might be a problem in Minneapolis or Baltimore but not in St. Luke. Clearly Victor had his own interest at heart, not that of St. Luke. He was overly influenced by the *Wall Street Journal*, corporate big-wigs, and other greedy business types.

Ken Keegan enjoyed his breakfast with Victor. While the two were not social friends, they were among the power-elite in St. Luke and often worked together on community issues. Ken knew all about Aclare from articles in *Education Week*. He understood Victor's concerns about the quality of high school graduates, especially those in the lower half of the class, who were more likely to stay in town and work at Gram Industries. His greatest concern was that Victor had not counseled with him earlier about seeing Jack Taylor and his Aclare Learning as a way to improve St. Luke High School. Ken learned that Victor had planned to talk with him immediately after Taylor's visit to St. Luke, but Taylor's speeding ticket placed things into motion faster than Victor had planned.

Ken had climbed the ranks in the public schools with administrative posts in Kimball and Foley before moving to St. Luke. He would give all he had to St. Luke while he was superintendent. The community might be best known for its football team, but Ken Keegan was a dedicated educator and nobody's fool.

He was relieved to learn that Victor wasn't interested in Aclare taking over the management of the entire school district as it had done in Annapolis and Syracuse. Ken knew all about the private management of public schools and was ready to place his Minnesota Ed.D. up against any Harvard MBA when it came to running a school district. Victor's desire for smarter graduates to run his machines was a familiar issue for him. He was pleased to hear that Victor wanted to see Aclare as an optional pilot program in the high school. The Aclare program would address what Victor needed in new employees: stronger math and reading abilities, and improved problem solving and critical thinking skills.

While Ken was relieved that Victor wasn't proposing a private management takeover, adopting the Aclare program would create a dilemma. Ken could easily be a warrior against a private takeover and indeed be seen as a hero among educators. Allowing the Aclare program to operate in St. Luke would prove more difficult. By opposing it, he would be up against Victor and the town's financial life blood. Opposition would be seen as defensive, as his unwillingness to try new methods and innovations. By supporting it, he would incur the wrath of the teachers' association and likely the scorn of many of his fellow superintendents.

Ken was a realist. The decision truly wasn't his. It belonged to the school board, but the board would look to him for an opinion, if not guidance. He knew that, of the seven school board members, two would undoubtedly oppose Aclare, two would support Victor, and three were hard to predict. Victor didn't ask for Ken's endorsement over breakfast, and Ken didn't offer it. It would take three board meetings for a vote. At the first meeting, Ken could legitimately defer his opinion to further study. But the clock was ticking. *The* Jack Taylor was coming back to town.

Chapter 4

# Monday of the Third Week of Football Season

"For crapsake, this is all we need," Carl grumbled, "We've got Elk River on Friday night, and the only thing this town is talking about is Aclare Learning. What the hell was your father-in-law thinking when he brought up this insane idea during football season?"

"For crapsake, Carl, I don't know. He didn't seek my advice."

David's parody of Carl brought instant relief. Carl bellowed a hearty laugh as he sat down behind his desk, took off his cap, and ran his fingers through his thinning hair. David sat on the sofa across from Carl and, with his left arm, tossed a football as close as he could to the ceiling without touching it. It had been a dismal Monday practice.

"I didn't see anything out there that I liked today. Those Elk River boys know how to play football. We don't play these guys every year, and this game scares me more than any on our schedule. Thank goodness it's a home game."

"Yeah, but Friday night the fans won't be watching the game; they'll be sitting in the stands reading Aclare's annual report."

"Yeah," Carl groused, "and callin' their damn brokers."

\* \* \*

Monday night at the Tuckers' was intense. Between discussing Aclare and Carl's worry about Elk River, the evening ran longer than usual. Bobbie was wound like a top. "You know, I understand,

Katy, what your father is worried about. So goes Gram Industries, so goes St. Luke."

"I think it's bigger than that for Dad," added Katy. "So goes Gram Industries, so goes America."

"That seems a bit overdramatic."

"Not if you listen to Dad. He's convinced that America's lost its competitive edge. Gram Industries is just a single example, but magnify it a thousand times or ten thousand times across the country, and you've got the situation. It's not just a matter of labor cost; it's about environmental protection, fair trade, Chinese currency props, industrial espionage, patent piracy. The labor issue, having smarter and more intellectually curious workers, is the one string Dad can play locally."

"But how can Aclare Learning help? I don't see the connection." Bobbie frowned.

"I'm not sure I do either. Everything I'm saying about Gram Industries comes from years of conversations with Dad. He hasn't asked or told me anything about Aclare. If I hadn't stumbled into his meeting with Jack Taylor, I would have learned about it with everyone else in Friday's *Leader.*

"Still," Bobbie persisted, "what's the connection between Aclare and the changing global economy? I'm not blind to what's going on around the world. I'm sure your father feels tremendous pressure from low-wage manufacturers. Blue-collar work migrates to the cheapest labor market. You can't buy anything at Wal-Mart that isn't made in China. All the electronics in this house and in St. Luke schools are made in Asia. Nearly every stitch of clothes I own was made in some Third World location, the wine we're having tonight is from Australia, the gas station at the highway is British Petroleum, Credit Suisse holds our brokerage account. We spend every spring break in Mexico. I drive a Toyota, and Carl has a Honda. I know we live in a global economy. Everyone knows we live in a global economy."

Bobbie ranted on. She pushed the hair away from her face with the back of her hand, still holding a paring knife, and looked at Katy,

"What the hell does all that have to do with Jack Taylor wanting to screw with St. Luke's schools?"

Katy didn't respond to the question, and Bobbie stood still for a moment. She placed the paring knife on the cutting board and said as much to herself as to Katy, "I like things the way they are. I understand them and do a decent job of controlling them. I don't want Jack Taylor threatening my world, getting his nose under the tent, mucking about for the wrong reasons. I don't want Bruce Barnes around here either. This school district is the best thing going for St. Luke. I feel like a TSA bag checker at a four-gate airport. The skies were only as safe as the least secure airport. Taylor isn't going to get into Minnesota via St. Luke."

"Are you okay?" Katy asked in response to Bobbie's flushed face and perspiring brow.

"Yeah," Bobbie composed herself. "I think I just had an Aclare moment. That SOB Taylor is not getting into St. Luke. I love you, Katy, and your father's company is in a difficult spot. My God, look at what I've just said about where all the things we buy come from. But Taylor's no solution. He's an opportunist, a capitalist mole, a mouse. I'm not afraid of mice, but I don't want them in my house. Jack Taylor is not gaining a foothold in St. Luke."

"But you haven't even heard him speak yet. He's not trying to take over the district. It's just a program, probably just a pilot test to see if Aclare gets better results for the students."

"That's his Trojan Horse, Katy. He'll sell whatever he can to get in. Once inside he'll spread like a cancer."

"Bobbie, you sound like Bruce Barnes. You've tried and convicted Taylor without his ever doing anything in St. Luke."

The paring knife slapped sharply against the cutting board. Bobbie shuddered. "Please don't compare me to Bruce Barnes," she said tightly. Again she collected herself and continued. "Katy, you always try to find the best in any situation. You have no worries. You have a fine husband, a beautiful daughter, and, for goodness sake, you're heir to the Gram fortune. Public schooling is a hobby interest for you."

Katy winced. "Bobbie, how can you say that?"

"That's the way it is, Katy," Bobbie said. "For Carl and me public schooling is everything. We've given our all for St. Luke and it's given us a good life in return." She sighed deeply. "I think I'll have some wine. Will you join me?"

"Certainly. Let's add to our great nation's trade deficit and raise a glass to the Aussie vintners."

"Hear, hear," responded Bobbie as their glasses clinked together. A moment passed. "So, how are things at Gram Industries, if I can ask without putting you in a difficult spot?"

Katy took a slow sip and paused a moment. Bobbie looked up from the cutting board, "That bad?"

"No," mused Katy. "Things are fine with the Grams and the locally legendary Gram fortune. I'm fourth-generation wealth, and time is surely on the side of money. I know it must look like my father is micro-managing the schools to grow his wealth, but that's not his intent. He doesn't need any more money. He's trying with all his might to help St. Luke."

"By inviting in a huckster like Taylor to yank up our skirts and boink us?"

"Bobbie, you're a raw nerve," Katy scolded. "I've never seen you like this before. Now calm down and listen. You must hold what I'm about to tell you in total confidence, just between you and me. Don't tell Carl because David doesn't even know this. Agreed?"

Bobbie paused, then dried her hands on a towel. "Agreed."

"Dad's has been staving off an offer from a South Korean firm to buy Gram Industries. They've been after him for almost two years. I love my father, but I don't want to run the business. And can you see David leading Gram? No, Dad's concerned that there's no successor to the throne. Because he's still in good health, he's been able to keep the buyers at bay."

"Why doesn't he sell it if you won't take it over, and God bless him for who he is, David's not suitable for the role? Couldn't he hire a manager?"

"To that last point, I can only say 'No way.' Dad lives with the ghosts of his father and grandfather. If the company's going to have the family name, it's got to have a Gram leading it."

"Okay, so no successor is apparent. Victor can't hold on until Anna finishes an MBA, so why not sell it? The new owner will carry on, and everything will be fine."

"If only it were that simple."

"What do you mean?"

"The South Koreans don't want to buy Gram Industries for its production quality. Instead, they want its long-term customer contacts and valued name among newspaper publishers. The Koreans will pay a premium for those relationships."

"I still don't see why Victor doesn't sell."

"Because once he sells and the Koreans assume relationships with Gram's customer base, the manufacturing will go to Asia. Dad says within two years of a sale, Gram Industries' facility in St. Luke will be shuttered."

"Oh, my goodness," Bobbie whispered. "That would ruin the town and the school district."

"I respect my father for what he's doing. He could sell the company and retire, not just wealthy but mega-wealthy. He'd be done with the worries and the fight to keep a Midwestern manufacturing company going when the odds are stacked against it. Bobbie, Dad's doing all he can for the people of St. Luke, not for Gram Industries. Making his company more competitive gives St. Luke a longer run, and, for reasons I don't know, he thinks Aclare can improve the odds of Gram Industries staying how it is and where it is."

"I never thought of that."

"My father may be the richest man in town, but he's also one of the most thoughtful. He truly feels that a better-educated workforce is needed to compete with Asia. Plus, it could buy more time for the company to stay in St. Luke."

"Your secret's safe with me," Bobbie heard herself say. "I feel mentally whiplashed. My opposition to Aclare could hasten the close of the financial lifeblood of St. Luke."

Carl and David were coming into the kitchen from the boat-house. "I tell you what, Carl," David teased, "this may be our last Monday of the season for watching film from the dock. I'm all for moving inside. It's getting too cold out there to enjoy my beer."

"Nonsense, never too cold to enjoy a beer. You're just a weenie. This is just a little cold snap. There'll be plenty of good Monday nights for fishing before football season's over." Carl and David sat down at the table. "Mother McCree, it sure smells good in here." Carl rubbed his hands together.

"I love serving enthusiastic eaters, but give me a few more minutes," Bobbie said. "Katy and I have been long on discussion and short on preparation."

"What?! Should my able assistant and I return to the warmth of the boathouse?"

"Hold your horses, Coach Lombardi. Just enjoy one another's company for a few minutes while Katy and I get supper on the table."

Carl and David looked at each another, stunned. "What's so important that supper got detained?" Carl asked.

Bobbie and Katy looked at each other, then Katy said, "Jack Taylor."

"Jeez 'O Pete, for crapsake, this guy's screwin' up my school, he's screwin' up my football team, and now he's screwin' up my supper. I've never met this turkey, but he's on my list. How can we help with supper?"

"Carl, shred the lettuce. David, keep an eye on the cheese bread. Take it out when it's browning and bubbling." Bobbie was quick to give orders and get Monday night back on track.

"I'll check Anna," Katy said. "Be right back."

Dinner was served. The conversation, however, stayed on the topic of the day. "So, what conclusions have you two reached on Jack Taylor?" Carl asked when the plates were full.

"No conclusions, Carl, just initial observations," Katy offered.

"And?"

"Well, Bobbie sees little of value in Taylor's interest in St. Luke. I'm more open-minded. After all, my daddy's the guy behind this."

"With all due respect to your father's wisdom and contributions to St. Luke, he picked one hellavu time to trot out this Taylor guy. Couldn't he have waited until after football season?"

"I doubt seriously, Carl, if Dad considered the athletic season's schedule in his planning."

"Shows how much he knows about public schooling."

"What do you mean?"

"Well, a good superintendent, or board member, or high-powered big-wig like your dad should never introduce a controversial measure during football season. And if they've got any brains in their heads, they won't do it during basketball season either."

"Are you serious?" Katy asked, slack-jawed.

"Damn right I am. Any controversy takes attention away from sports, and sports hold schools and communities together. People don't come together on Friday nights to watch a math test. They don't come to the gym to discuss a book. They come to watch sports. They come to be entertained, to dominate the other towns in the area, to support their kids on the team, in the band, on cheering squads, and to whoop it up in the stands. They come for community. To remember their youth. To celebrate their children. Sports, my dearest ones, is the glue that holds American public education together. Take sports away and the Jack Taylors of this country will steal the schools from the people."

* * *

AS THEY LAY IN BED LATER that night, Katy asked David if he agreed with Carl that sports hold schools together.

"You know, for all the years I played football, I never thought of that. I just saw sports as part of the curriculum—or the extracurriculum. But Carl's point sure makes sense. If you took football and basketball away, I don't think communities would care as much about their schools.

At Iowa I knew that winning teams meant money for the university, not just gate receipts from Kinnick Stadium but an overall pride and positive spirit that encouraged giving from friends and alumni. I guess it's the same thing at the high school level. Winning teams help the school and the school district. If the community is proud of its schools, the community's more likely to support the school, pass the levies, and tax themselves so the goodness goes on."

"Sports certainly didn't hold my boarding school together," Katy said. "St. Genevieve was held together by money, elitism, and religious isolationists. Not to mention gender isolationists and a strong mistrust of males."

"Wow, that's a pretty condemning description. I've never heard you talk about St. Gen that way."

"You know, I've never thought of it that way until right now. Carl's statement about sports and schools really hit me. I think he's right. If the Lettermen didn't dominate in football, do you think this town would be as supportive of the schools? I doubt it. St. Luke would be more like the very towns it feels so superior to. That says a lot about the role of football. I'm flabbergasted. I've never connected the dots before. It's like it's been right under my nose—under all our noses—for years, but we've never seen it. Or if we've seen it, we've never discussed it. Like an elephant in the room."

"Sounds like Jack Taylor's visit has you thinking."

"Something has," Katy said. She pulled David's hand in hers as she rolled over.

Chapter 5

# Friday of the Third Week and Tuesday of the Fourth Week of Football Season

THE LETTERMEN WERE FLAT, distracted, and failing to execute. Carl Tucker was beside himself. As he paced the sidelines, time after time he heard the fans behind him: "Going to the board meeting this week? . . . Wouldn't miss it . . . What do you think the board's going to say to this Jack Taylor guy?"

"For crapsake," Carl bellowed to David as they stood on the sidelines, "we've got a major team up here for a home game, they're eating our lunch, and our fans are talking about the school board meeting!"

In the fourth quarter the score was the only thing that didn't indicate how dominant the opposition was. Elk River had twice the first downs and total yardage and had controlled the ball nearly the entire game. The Lettermen had scored all their points in the third quarter on a pass from midfield only because the Elk River defender had fallen. The score going into the final minutes was 14 to 7.

On a third and eight play, Elk River was in a passing situation. One more first down and they could run the clock out. The Lettermen defense showed blitz, and the quarterback yelled an audible as he set under center. The St. Luke fans had finally focused on the game and were making such a noise that the Elk River left end missed the audible. When the quarterback dropped back three quick steps and fired the ball, it was right into the hands of the Lettermen defensive end, who took the ball into the end zone untouched.

The stadium erupted as Coach Tucker held up two fingers and screamed into David's ear, "I'm calling the drop play. We haven't moved the ball at all on the ground. This is it, David. This is the season."

The St. Luke fans quieted as the team broke the huddle. Elk River fans screamed for all they were worth to keep *their* perfect season intact. David looked at Carl. This play could mean retirement for Carl or another year or maybe several more before he would have a chance to retire with a perfect season. Tears welled in David's eyes, caught in the emotion of the significance of what was about to happen. David had drilled his players dozens of times on the drop pass. His confidence was high that they would execute, but his heart was heavy. A successful two-point conversion would put Carl's retirement dream in full motion, and David would ascend as head coach.

David continued to watch Carl as the play unfolded. The jubilation all around him told him that the play had worked, but Carl's face didn't change; he stood frozen with his players dancing around him. David's eyes welled again, but he shook himself and got the kickoff team on the field and rallied the defense to hold off Elk River's two-minute drill.

After shaking hands at midfield with the Elk River coaches, Carl put his arm around David and said, "We were lucky, damned lucky tonight. Elk River whipped our fanny, but it's a smooth road ahead for the rest of the season. I'll announce a week before the season final. For crapsake, I'm gonna miss this game."

"You know, you don't have to go, Carl," David said seriously as they walked off the field.

"No, the stars are aligning. I want to go out with a perfect season, and I don't want to wait around for another one. I might be an old man by then."

\* \* \*

THE ELK RIVER GAME was overshadowed by the coming board meeting. While it was not a pretty win, stolen not earned, Carl remained ruffled that his Lettermen had to share the stage with a jerk named Jack Taylor. So it was with a combination of curiosity and annoyance that Carl attended the school board meeting.

Carl entered the meeting a full half hour after it had started. He took the last open seat in the room, the one right behind David. The routine business was not the draw tonight. Bobbie, as association head, was seated in the front. Ken Keegan sat with the district's book-keeper at a table opposite the board members.

St. Luke had turned out. The room overflowed with the opinionated and the curiosity seekers. Katy was home with Anna, and Victor was out of town on business. As the board was concluding its old business, Jack Taylor entered a side door, a buzz went through the room and all eyes stared at a relaxed, confident, and smiling man neatly dressed and alone. David had expected several curriculum and finance people in tow, a slide presentation—a full-court press to make his point. Despite being solo, Taylor was obviously comfortable. Taylor had been screamed at, spat upon, pelted with garbage, protested against, and physically pushed and shoved at school board meetings up and down the East Coast where he had offered Aclare Learning as an alternative to high drop-out rates, dismal test scores, uninspired teaching, union strangleholds, lethargic bureaucracies, and disengaged students. He sat down in St. Luke to the whisper of small town people excited to see him.

Two minutes hadn't passed when Board Chair Douglas Nickerson moved the agenda to New Business. Nickerson paused for a moment and looked at the packed room. "Well, I know you didn't come here tonight to hear the budget report." There were chuckles as people adjusted themselves in their seats. "We are all mighty proud of our schools and our kids in St. Luke. But I'm sure you've read *The Leader* and are interested in hearing from our out-of-town guest tonight. It's too bad Victor Gram isn't here this evening. His business relationship with Mr. Taylor has brought about Aclare Learning's interest in St. Luke."

"We don't need him here!" someone shouted from the back row. The outcry started restless discussion across the room. Nickerson squelched the bubbling uproar. "Now ladies and gentlemen, Mr. Taylor is here to address the board and this community on a very important matter. We will be courteous and give him the respect he deserves."

"Why do we need him here? We beat Elk River last week, didn't we, Coach?"

Carl winced at the inappropriateness of the comment.

Nickerson stood up. "I'm not going to stand for this. The room will come to order, or I will have it cleared, and only the board will hear Mr. Taylor." Immediately, the crowd quieted. "Now, Mr. Taylor, welcome to St. Luke. Victor Gram is certainly a leading figure in this community, and if he thinks what you have to say is important, then this board will listen and give all due consideration. Would you please state your full name, place of residence, and purpose of your appearance at the board meeting."

The room was dead silent. "John Francis Taylor. I live in San Francisco. I'm here at the request of Victor Gram, who would like to see the programs of my company, Aclare Learning, adopted in St. Luke."

"Thank you, Mr. Taylor. This is not a courtroom. The name and place of residence are just the way we like to get started. The board has reviewed the materials you sent in advance of this meeting. We're gathering a list of questions for you and references from other school districts back East where your company is working. Those questions will come to you early next week. Two weeks from tonight we've scheduled a formal presentation from your company to this board. Tonight we welcome your remarks and will have an open microphone for any teachers or community members to ask you questions. Again, I welcome you."

There was another shifting in the seats as Nickerson opened the floor to Taylor, who waited for the rustle of the crowd to die down before beginning. "Thank you, Chairman Nickerson, for your welcome and for laying out the course of the upcoming board meeting. As we both noted, I'm here at the urging of Victor Gram. Victor and I were introduced by a friend in Chicago. Victor seems to think that Aclare Learning would benefit St. Luke High School and, subsequently, Gram Industries. I would like to take a few minutes tonight to tell you what Aclare Learning does and how it does it, so that the board and community can assess if St. Luke can benefit. Tonight's presentation is from me, my thoughts, my vision, my company. With that in mind, I'd like to stand and address both the board and the community. After all, I assume most of those in this crowded room are parents or teachers who have a great deal of love and concern for the young people of St. Luke."

Taking the microphone from its stand, Taylor faced the room. Unlike the inner city parents he was used to addressing, he looked out upon all white faces. Seed caps and camouflage were abundant. Heavy work boots poked into the aisles from the legs of those tired from the day's harvest. The faces were not hostile. They were open, respectful, and edged toward eagerness. There may have been a couple of outbursts that Chairman Nickerson quelled, but this group seemed plainer and far more polite than any he had ever addressed.

"Thank you for coming. It shows that you care about your children, your schools, and your community. I haven't spent much time in Minnesota, but from my few trips here, I've found the people very kind and pleasant. This state has a reputation in our nation of being a place of good schools and clean government, of hardworking, noncomplaining, tough people who live in a land of great beauty and harsh winters. And although I've not experienced them, I believe Minnesota also claims the mosquito as its state bird and fishing as its official religion." That lightened the mood of the room ever so slightly.

"I'm honored to be here. I take the responsibility of educating young men and women of this country very seriously, and though you may not know much about Aclare Learning and may be suspicious of it or even hostile toward it, I ask you to listen before you judge, and judge on evidence, not on rumors.

"But, first, let me speak about one of my favorite topics, me." Genuine laughter erupted from the room. "As you might surmise from my name, John Francis, I am Catholic, a cradle Catholic if you will. I was born where I still live, in San Francisco. I had a typical middle-class upbringing—Jesuit Catholic schooling, a paper route, and three years at the Safeway, the grocery store near our home. I was fortunate to win a scholarship and receive an excellent college education at Dartmouth. I am married. I married above myself to a woman I think is the finest human being in the world—Rebecca, the mother of our six beautiful children." When he said six children, there was a palpable relaxation in the room.

Taylor spoke for fifteen minutes. He focused on his business story: made a bundle in the heyday of Silicon Valley, took time off to consider what to do next, conveniently avoided losing his shirt in the tech crash, and decided to devote the next phase of his life to improving America's public schools. He named the company Aclare after the village his maternal great-grandmother left in County Sligo during the famine in Ireland.

There was a hush over the school board meeting. Jack Taylor worked the crowd. He had made eye contact with every person in the room, including school board members. He connected with them. But David felt there was something too polished about him, too perfect.

Taylor described the development of Aclare. Buzz words and catch phrases bounced off of David's ears: the best and brightest minds created Aclare. Aclare gets far superior results. People are self-learners. Knowledge explosion. Self-paced. Continually updated. Critical thinking. Global competitiveness.

"Come on," David said leaning back to Carl. "This is a live infomercial. I'm not buying it."

"Aclare is a self-paced, continually updated learning system that allows students to advance rapidly in their knowledge of the world and their critical-thinking skills, two areas vital if America's to compete in a global economy."

David leaned back again, and mouthed, "Bullshit."

"You can hear the passion in my voice. I'm proud of Aclare. It offers high school students and, subsequently, this nation, a dramatic improvement in knowledge acquisition and critical thinking. I completely understand why Victor Gram wants Aclare in St. Luke schools. With Aclare, those students who leave high school to work at Gram Industries will be more in tune with a global economy and more capable of competing on the world stage."

There was a slight pause as Jack Taylor shifted from evangelical mode and prepared for the question-and-answer period. "I'll remind you that two weeks from tonight I'll be back here with my colleagues to address the specifics of what Aclare does and discuss its strong track record. But for now, I'll do my very best to answer your questions."

The crowd sat motionless. The heckling that Taylor had heard at the beginning of his spot on the agenda did not portend a rush to the microphone to denounce him and his kind. After a thirty-second period in which people collected their thoughts and tried to remember why they had come to shout down Jack Taylor, Grace Everson, a retired teacher, broke the ice and walked to the microphone for comments by the public.

The room settled as Grace adjusted the microphone to her five-foot-two frame. She cleared her throat directly into the microphone, then said, "Mr. Taylor, I had not expected such a personal and passionate presentation from you tonight, and though many of us here are Lutherans, we're still capable of being moved by strong rhetoric. Nonetheless, as you'll find, we Lutherans are a grounded people and will ask you endless practical questions. Let me ask you this," Grace went on, "how can you, a businessman, be a leader of an education company?"

Jack smiled and drew a long breath. "No, I'm not a teacher. I've never taken a class at a university on teaching. But I'll say two things in response to your question, Mrs. Everson. First, for the most part, the seven men and two women behind me, the St. Luke School Board, are not teachers either, but they are ultimately in charge of the school district. That's somewhat of a parallel to me and Aclare Learning. Below me is a bevy of talented teachers and technology experts who develop the Aclare product. As CEO, I let them run, do their thing, while I work to get the results of their labor into school districts. Second, sometimes it can be helpful to have people not raised in a system to observe that system and offer suggestions for improvement. Whether in our families, or our businesses, or our churches, for that matter, it can be good to open the windows and let in fresh air. You're right. I'm not an educator; I'm a businessman working to improve education in America."

Two people clapped at Taylor's remarks but quickly stopped when others didn't join in.

The ice was broken. Taylor took fifteen minutes of questions until Chairman Nickerson spoke up. "Ladies and gentlemen, I'm going to cut off the questions. Mr. Taylor and his associates will be here again in two weeks. At that time we plan to adjust the agenda to allow a full review of Aclare Learning. Mr. Taylor, thank you for your remarks, and we look forward to your return."

"Chairman Nickerson, if I may, I have a very brief closing remark."

"Of course, Mr. Taylor."

"Ladies and gentlemen, a week from tonight Aclare Learning will have its shareholders' meeting at the Pacific Pass Hotel in San Francisco. I welcome your attendance to learn more about the company. If you would like to attend, I will leave all the information needed with Chairman Nickerson."

David laughed as he turned to Carl. "Who in this room would go to San Francisco for an Aclare shareholders' meeting? Taylor's drawn an unnecessary divide between his world and ours. No one will fly to San Francisco. Taylor's nuts."

David went right home after the meeting and found Katy anxious to hear how it had gone. David gave a blow-by-blow description of the presentation and finished with Taylor's foolish invitation to the shareholders' meeting.

"Why is the invitation so foolish?" Katy asked.

"Who from St. Luke would go?"

"You, with my dad."

Chapter 6

# *Tuesday of the Fifth Week of Football Season*

IT WASN'T JUST VICTOR AND DAVID who met on Tuesday morning at the St. Cloud airport where the Gram Industries jet was kept. Victor had made certain that all eight passenger seats were filled. Also along to San Francisco were School Board Chairman Douglas Nickerson, Superintendent Ken Keegan, School Board Member Melvin Vilsak, Science Department Chair Sharon Lunsford, Monsignor Patrick Murphy of St. Ansgar Catholic Church, and Bobbie Tucker.

As the pilots went through their preflight checks on the tarmac, David considered his fellow passengers. How had each become part of the St. Luke delegation to the Aclare shareholders' meeting? David knew why he was here. He was Victor's son-in-law, but as an English teacher and assistant football coach, the least influential person in the entourage.

David clearly understood why Doug Nickerson, Ken Keegan, and Bobbie were along. He was curious, though, how Melvin Vilsak had been chosen from the school board members. He was known for his pedantic ravings at school board meetings over the tiniest issues. He was narrow and cold and regarded by most in St. Luke as a pain in the ass. Perhaps he was taking the seat that the high school principal, Stewart Johnson, would have had were he not presenting at a conference in Chicago. Perhaps he was the only board member available for the trip, but David recalled that his brother, Rudy, worked at Gram Industries and wondered if that was why he was on the flight.

42

As chair of the Science Department and an active member of the association, Sharon Lunsford's participation in the trip was not unexpected. But she was the youngest department chair in the high school, and David knew there were any number of more experienced faculty members who could have made the trip in her place. He concluded that it must be her science background that made her the association's pick. He looked at her trying not to stare. She seemed quite different. She was sharply dressed in slacks, a tweed jacket, and heels. David had always considered her mousey and bookish, with thick glasses, bulky sweaters, and severely pulled-back hair. The difference was night and day. Today she looked strong, comfortable, and confident.

The only passenger without a direct connection to either Gram Industries or the school district was Monsignor Murphy. Although St. Luke had a few more Lutherans than Catholics, Monsignor Patrick Murphy was the most influential clergyman in town. Murphy was at the tail end of the flood of Irish priests recruited, sent, and cajoled to serve the Catholic Church in America. As a child, David had attended St. Lucy's, the parish and elementary school on the working-class side of town. St. Ansgar's had always been the more affluent Catholic church. After David married Katy, it had taken only a short time to feel at home in his new parish. Monsignor Murphy had gone out of his way to make David feel welcome.

David knew it was the Gram connection that had gotten him the attention. Had he not been married to Katy and simply had switched parishes, he would have been just be another set of cheeks in a pew. But he had looked beyond Monsignor's attention to him as an in-law of the Grams and had developed a genuine liking for the aged Irishman, whom David regarded as the best read and keenest mind in St. Luke. David was pleased that Monsignor Murphy was a part of the trip. Murphy would be a touchstone for Victor and an ambassador for St. Luke.

Chairman Nickerson addressed the passengers as the plane taxied to the end of the runway. "Well, I guess I've got to say this, Melvin, you and I can't discuss any school board business. Silly as that sounds, we'd be violating the trust of the people of St. Luke according to Minnesota's open-meeting law. So, Melvin, we can talk fishing, hunting, booze, and women, and we won't be a disappointment to St. Luke, but talk about school business and we'll be the shame of the community."

Everyone laughed and the engine roared. David watched the ground as the plane crossed Highway 10 and gained altitude over the campus of St. Cloud State. Quickly the plane climbed above the clouds, and David closed his eyes and enjoyed the inactivity. He could hear the others talking. Monsignor and Keegan were discussing Thanksgiving; Ken's two sons would be home from the University of St. Thomas in St. Paul. Nickerson and Melvin were having no trouble avoiding district business. They were discussing recipes for venison sausage. Victor and Bobbie were barely audible as they reviewed the itinerary for the trip. Sharon was reading as David drifted to sleep.

Victor had two cars meet the group at the San Francisco airport, and they arrived at the Pacific Pass Hotel just before two. The reception, the opening event at the shareholder's meeting, started at five. David checked into his room, unpacked, and went for a swim. Despite his lopsided stroke, David loved to swim, and few activities stretched his shoulder in quite such a pleasantly painful way. He was the only one in the pool on that weekday afternoon when Sharon Lunsford came in, wearing the terry cloth guest robe found in each room. David had stopped for a breath at the deep end of the pool when Sharon dropped her robe. David was stunned. Why had he never noticed Sharon's figure before?

Sharon walked the length of the pool, her hair back in a pony tail and her figure bouncing with each footfall of her bare feet. She stood with her toes over the edge of the deep end of the pool. Just as she sprang for her dive, she noticed David and screamed as she hit the water.

As she came up, David said, "Sharon, are you all right?"

Confused, Sharon took a moment and asked cautiously, "David, is that you?"

"Yes, are you all right?"

"Oh, I'm so grateful it's you. I thought I was alone, and just as I dove, I noticed you out of the corner of my eye, and . . . I don't know why . . . I screamed."

"Don't worry, I got here a bit ago and was just catching my breath. I slept most of the flight and thought a swim would clear my head. I've done quite a few laps, so I'll leave and you can have the pool to yourself."

"Oh, no. Now that I know it's you, please stay."

It seemed a strange statement to David, but he was pleased to stay. He was still amazed by Sharon's transformation.

"I don't have my contacts in, and I took my glasses off just as I came through the door. I'm blind as a bat."

"Don't worry. Katy's the same way. But she doesn't scream at the sight of me, at least not very often."

Sharon laughed and swam toward David. She treaded with her chin just above the water. For a moment David didn't know what to say. Inside the high school, or even running into her at the grocery store, there was always something to talk about. But here, out of their element and alone in their swimsuits, David worked harder than needed to strike up a conversation. "So, how did you get to be part of this trip to San Francisco?" *Oh great*, David thought, *what in insulting question. I'm here because my father-in-law owns the jet. My question seems to accuse a fellow teacher of not having the credentials or connections to be part of the delegation.*

"You know, that's a good question, David. The only thing I can tell you is the truth. The association asked me to make the trip. I was surprised to be asked. I'm fairly active in the association, but there are lots of teachers senior to me who could be here. But a trip to San Francisco! And during the school week! Wow! I jumped at the chance."

David was drawn to Sharon's candor. "Are you supposed to make a report afterwards?"

"No, I was told to keep my eyes open and ask lots of questions. That's pretty much what I tell my kids in science to do. So I guess I can practice what I teach."

Again, David was disarmed by Sharon's simple perspective. He relaxed, and they swam and then hung on the side of the pool and talked for half an hour. David wondered why he and Katy hadn't grown closer to

Sharon in her three years in the district. She was interesting: an Army brat, born and raised for twelve years in South Korea, bounced around the States with her military family through high school, a double major in biology and physics from Wisconsin, married right out of college and divorced two years later. Her parents and several siblings had settled in western Wisconsin. Sharon took a teaching position in St. Luke to be near enough to them but far enough from them while she thought about other ways to use her science skills. Her parents were in good health but she treasured her numerous nieces and nephews whom she showered with attention.

As they were drying off, still talking, Sharon slipped on the wet floor while putting on one of her sandals and fell forward. David instinctively grabbed her, and she immediately wrapped her arms around him for support. "Thank you," she said, "In addition to being blind, I'm also a klutz. I nearly took a header putting on my shoe. That would've been great, going to the meeting tonight with a black eye and stitches in my head." As David relaxed his support of her, he noticed Melvin Vilsak looking at them through a hallway window. David waved to Melvin, who didn't wave back but just walked away.

"No problem," David said as Sharon put on her robe and they headed to the elevator. They bantered and laughed all the way to the fourth floor, "Okay, okay, let me get a grip," Sharon said. "Now, what time does this begin, and where do we go?"

"Everything's here in the hotel. At five there's the reception, and at 6:30 there's the Aclare Rally. I'm not sure what to expect from either. Tomorrow is the shareholders' meeting. They're all on the mezzanine level."

"I'll knock on your door at five, and we'll go down together. What's your room number?"

"It's 415. Hey, when do we eat? I'm starving. My stomach's still on Central Time."

"Mine too, but don't pig out at the reception. Remember, Victor's taking us all to his favorite Chinatown restaurant."

# Chapter 7

# *Tuesday Evening of the Fifth Week of Football Season*

Two taps on door 415, and Sharon opened quickly. "Come in. I've just got to put on my shoes, but don't worry, you won't have to catch me this time." David stepped into the room; Sharon sat on the side of the bed and fastened the straps of her heels. Sixty seconds later they exited Sharon's room just as Melvin was rounding the corner. "Hello," Melvin said rather coolly as they stepped into the elevator.

"Hey, are we all on the fourth floor?" Sharon asked.

"I'm in 437. Victor's across the hall in 436. Nickerson's on the seventh floor. I don't know about the others. What room are you in, David?"

"Uh . . . 407"

"How's the view?"

"Don't know. I haven't looked out the window."

The elevator doors opened on the mezzanine level. Melvin stepped out quickly. Sharon and David looked at another with a "What's with him?" expression. They followed the flow of people into a ballroom and were surprised to see that even though it was just a few minutes after five, there were already several hundred people at the reception. The ballroom was spacious and elegant like the rest of the hotel. Two chandeliers provided warm and comfortable lighting, and a buzz of laughter and earnest talk filled the room. Three bars along the perimeter offered refreshment, and a squadron of white-jacketed servers circulated with trays of delicacies. "May I get you something to drink?" David asked Sharon.

"Please."

David returned and handed Sharon a glass of wine. "Whatever this is, it's mighty good."

A moment later, Monsignor Murphy stepped up and said, "David, I hate to steal your lovely companion, but, Sharon, would you please join me? There's the most interesting conversation going about Aclare's science curriculum, and I think you'd love to hear it. Excuse us please, David."

As David surveyed the room, he saw Victor speaking with Jack Taylor. He walked toward them. Victor raised his hand to Jack in a "hold that thought" motion and said, "David, David, come join us. I want you to meet Jack. Jack, this is my son-in-law, David Anderson. David, Jack Taylor."

As the men shook hands, David was aware of Victor looking at them intently, almost as if to see who was taller. While pleased that Victor had welcomed him into the conversation, David was surprised. He knew Victor still carried the feeling that Katy could have done better, specifically, that she could have married a man of wealth and social stature. Nonetheless, David and Jack were rolling in conversation. "So you're Katy's husband and Anna's father? You have a beautiful wife and daughter."

"Thank you. I'm a lucky man. How do you think your presentation was received in St. Luke?"

"I think it went reasonably well. St. Luke proved a good audience. It was different from what I usually face. But, more importantly, what did you think of it?"

"Well, I was expecting a lot more glitz, more numbers, more razzle-dazzle. But your simple introduction of who you are and what Aclare does went a long way with the audience. No slide show or marketing presentation could have done as much as your talk to increase your footing in St. Luke. A tip of the cap to your instincts. When you told St. Luke that you had six children, you were welcomed within our very conservative Catholic community."

48

Taylor seemed taken aback, "I had no idea. I didn't realize the size of my family merited bonus points in St. Luke. Here in California among my friends the size of my family is seen as a quaint anomaly, tolerated but not encouraged, so to speak." Taylor took a sip of wine and brought the conversation back to David's critique. "Other thoughts on my presentation?"

David added, "I was less enamored by the deluge of buzz words. Education is full of them, but your talk had too many, too much jargon, too many superlatives. Simpler claims, simpler language was called for in my opinion."

"Thank you for your candor. Actually, I hadn't planned to be there alone. My razzle-dazzle team was already occupied. We have two teams that present before school boards, but one was in Charleston and the other in Cleveland, so I came alone. I don't know if it was instinct, but without my marketing team, I told the only story I have."

"That story was based on truth, your truth, your story, and no one could dispute it. There was a lot of hostility in that room before you spoke, and your personal story disarmed it. The people of St. Luke will care about your data and the proof that Aclare works. They will not be an easy sell, but you got to first base with that fifteen-minute talk. You may be from out of town, but you're not a stranger anymore and that'll make a critical difference."

Jack looked at Victor. "How come this guy isn't working for you? He seems to possess two ingredients seldom found in American business, candor and simplicity."

Victor was uncharacteristically speechless. He looked at David and then Jack and said, "I don't know."

"Well, let me tell you this," Jack took a sip of wine, "son-in-law or no son-in-law, if you—"

The conversation was interrupted by a lovely woman with red hair. "Mr. Taylor, we need you in the auditorium. It will just take a few minutes."

"Sorry, Victor, but I've got to attend to some razzle-dazzle, as David calls it." Jack shook hands with Victor, then David. "I look forward to continuing our conversation." He was whisked through the crowded room with people catching his eye, waving, and shouting his name as he passed.

Victor looked at David, but before he could speak, Douglas Nickerson, Ken Keegan, and Bobbie appeared. "Well, we're just getting started, but what do you think?" Victor asked.

Keegan spoke first. "I haven't been to a big ballroom reception like this since last year's Minnesota Superintendent Association meeting at Madden's in Brainerd. Let me make this clear: I still don't have an opinion on Aclare, but I have two observations between that superintendents' meeting and this Aclare thing. First, there's a lot more talk about education at this meeting, and second, the wine's a damn sight better."

"I'll second the second observation, Ken," injected Nickerson. "Great wine."

"Yes, the wine is lovely," added Bobbie, "but I can't get over the size of that Aclare banner hanging on the wall. For goodness sake, it's bigger than the scoreboard at Letterman Field."

As everyone laughed, David excused himself and grabbed Bobbie's arm to work the room with her. They met a gentleman who was a portfolio manager for the Retired Teachers Association of Florida. Aclare was a part of their portfolio. David asked if there wasn't a contradiction in investing retired teachers' money in a company that the teachers' associations hated. He responded, "That's not an issue for us. My group's job is to produce the best return for our clients within their risk parameters. Aclare meets risk tolerance for our clients, in this case the Florida retired teachers. My group likes the trajectory of the stock. Taylor's a back-able guy. We understand the political volatility of what he's doing. If his situation becomes adverse, we'll get out. But right now, his company is making a lot of money for our clients."

An elderly black woman stopped David and Bobbie and introduced herself as Viola Fulghum. Viola asked what had brought them to the Aclare reception. When David told her, she said, "Do it, young man. Bring Aclare to your town in Minnesota. Don't think twice; don't look back. Just move forward."

David was puzzled. "Why are you so passionate about Aclare?"

"Let me tell you this, young man. I am from Richmond, Richmond, Virginia. I live on Social Security. This is my third Aclare event, and I hope to have a hundred more. I do this for my vacation every year. Wherever the Aclare meeting is, that's where I go. My son helps me some, but mostly I save my money for this to tell folks like you that Aclare saved my grandbaby.

"Four years ago, that boy was on the wrong track. He was a fifth grader in Annapolis but couldn't read the Lord's Prayer; he was getting an attitude, running with some wild young men. Then Mr. Taylor's company comes along, and that boy falls under Aclare's spell. He turns himself around. He flies right, studies hard. He spent two years in an Aclare school and then he was selected for the magnet math and science high school.

"He's now with good kids who care about their studies and will make something of themselves. There's no way he would have made it if weren't for Mr. Taylor. Before Aclare, nobody cared about that boy at school. He was just one more black face."

The diminutive, gray-haired grandmother took David's hand and looked into his eyes. "This man saves black children. He saves them from a system that doesn't expect or demand anything of them." Tears welled in her eyes. "I'm here to say that Mr. Taylor saved my grandbaby and there are millions of them to save."

She moved off with her cane into the crowd. David felt a rush of emotion: anger at the system, joy for Viola Fulghum, sympathy for kids trapped with no future, and admiration for Taylor for creating hope for Viola and her grandson. Bobbie leaned into David and whispered, "She's a fake, an actress Taylor pays to play that role. No woman on Social Security would attend these meetings regularly."

Out of the clutter of noise in the room, David focused on two voices directly behind him. He motioned to Bobbie to eavesdrop with him. "Taylor's trajectory is going off the chart. There's so much piling on this bubble that the stock's bound to pop. The PE is in the stratosphere.

Earnings will have to quintriple to bring the PE to twice the market's. We've ridden this puppy long enough. Unless there's something I'm not expecting at this event, I'll advise my clients to begin to sell their positions. No, run for the exits. Get out before the stampede."

They continued to mill about the room and engaged in conversations with anyone willing to talk, and it seemed everyone was willing to talk about some aspect of Aclare. It was Aclare that brought these people together, and they were here to support it and learn all they could about it. The atmosphere reminded David of gatherings of Hawkeye fans. Regardless of the sport or season of the year, Hawk fans enjoyed mixers, rallies, meetings with the coaches, or any other reason to get together to talk Iowa sports. Everyone in attendance had the common element of being an Iowa fan. So it was at this gathering. Bobbie and David were speaking with two Aclare curriculum designers who introduced the concept of string theory learning. As they were talking, David was distracted by the name badges worn by the two people right next to them. He was sure the name tags said the National Teachers Association and the American Federation of Educators. Overcome by curiosity, he excused himself from the curriculum women and pulled Bobbie with him.

"Hello, I'm David Anderson from the St. Luke Independent School District in Minnesota, and this is my colleague Bobbie Tucker." They shook hands with Tim Jenson and Sam Block. Seeming eager to talk, Jenson and Block asked what they were doing at an Aclare meeting. After explaining that they were part of a delegation from the district considering Aclare, they got smiling nods and, "There are probably a half dozen districts here, but you are certainly the smallest we've met."

"Yes, Aclare is in discussion with St. Luke due to a business relationship between Jack Taylor and one of the town's leading citizens," Bobbie noted, "but, may I ask, what brings the NTA and the AFE to this event?"

"It sounds like you're surprised we're here."

"Well, I am."

"Is St. Luke affiliated with the association or the federation?"

"We have members in both, but the association bargains for us, and I lead the local."

"Great, Bruce Barnes is one tough cookie. You can go back and tell him and all your colleagues that you saw some of their dues in action when you met us."

"I'll make sure I do that, but I'm still curious about you being here," Bobbie said.

"Well, there are two main reasons we attend the Aclare events, and, by the way, we do the same thing with every publicly traded company that works with schools, at least those that affect the lives of our members or the students—the food service companies, maintenance and janitorial companies, and the management and curriculum delivery companies. First, we're very concerned about salaries, wages, and working conditions. We don't like to see shareholders making money off our people's jobs; and second, we represent our organizations' interests in Aclare."

"You mean, the NTA and the AFE own stock in Aclare!" David exclaimed with a look of disbelief.

"Sure, but you're not alone. Most people are surprised to see us here and to learn that our organizations own a modest chunk of Aclare. But, when you think about it, meetings like this give us great intelligence on Aclare. We meet people like you, get a feeling for the momentum behind Aclare, hear shareholders' concerns at the meeting, and get time with Jack Taylor. It makes it easier to keep an eye on him."

"It sounds like your organizations have a conflict of interest. You'd like your investment to do well but you'd like the company you're invested in to do poorly. Am I right?" David said with a grin.

"Yeah, we'd gladly lose our shirts on the investment to see this threat to our members go belly-up. As a stock Aclare is now wildly speculative, thanks in part to ownership by us and many of our affiliates. We're helping to drive up demand for the equity. And we can help drive it down as well. All within the rules."

"But why does Aclare let you own shares?" Bobbie asked.

Sam laughed. "Aclare has no choice. It's Wall Street, the free market system. Ain't America great!?" David and Bobbie laughed along as a half dozen servers in white coats emerged, tapping triangles to announce it was time to move from the reception to the ballroom for the rally.

"David, Bobbie, it's great to meet you. I want to hustle in there to get a good seat. If the rally is anything like past years, you'll love it. Sometimes I don't know whether to laugh or cry."

"What do you mean?" asked David.

"Come and sit with us. I can tell you on the way."

"Thanks, but we've got to get back with some of our delegation."

"Then, in short, what you're about to experience is one part politics, one part marketing, a dash of Amway, and a lot of showmanship. Taylor loves to show off the great things Aclare does for kids, and in this era of data-driven decision making, Aclare's got the numbers. Its research is rigorous, and its results are damned impressive. Sure, Taylor builds his company on the troubles of his customers. But in this rally, he loves to bite the hand that feeds him. Look, we've got to run. I hear Paul Simon is his warm-up tonight. Hope we can hook up later."

The union reps moved off toward the ballroom doors as David and Bobbie looked around for others from St. Luke. Seeing no familiar faces, they were about to head into the ballroom when Monsignor Murphy came up. "I guess I chose the wrong time to go to the restroom. What happened? Looks like the party's over."

"No, Monsignor," Bobbie said, "I think the party might just be getting started."

"What?"

"While you were in the restroom, the ballroom doors were opened. You'd have thought this place was on fire as quickly as it cleared out. Let's go see what it's all about."

Chapter 8

# Tuesday Night of the Fifth Week of Football Season

THE ST. LUKE DELEGATION met in the hotel lobby after the rally. Victor had reserved a private room at the Silk Dragon, where he'd spent many hours in recent years meeting his Korean suitors and their American representatives. It was just a three-block walk from the Pacific Pass.

It was plain to see that Victor was a regular at the restaurant. Greeted with a bow and long handshake by the owner, Thomas Chin, Victor introduced David as his son but did not introduce the rest of the group. As they walked through the restaurant, David glanced back to make sure everyone was heading to the dining room prepared for them. He was surprised to see Sharon talking with Mr. Chin. David couldn't see Sharon's face, but he could see Mr. Chin speaking to her, but not in English. He watched as Sharon broke into laughter, then kissed the Chinese octogenarian on the cheek.

In the private dining room, David was seated at an oblong table between Sharon and Victor. In making the reservation, Victor had also made arrangements for Mr. Chin to provide an array of the house favorites. The group was famished. It was 8:30 Pacific time, a full four hours later than the usual meal time for the Minnesotans.

Almost immediately after being seated, drinks and appetizers were served. Victor leaned over to David. "Well, son, what did you think?"

Victor had never called David "son" in his five years of marriage to Katy. After quickly absorbing the change in status from son-in-law to son, David responded, "To borrow a line from Pogo, 'We have met the enemy and he is us.'"

Victor broke out laughing and slapped David on the back. "That great line from Walt Kelly can be applied in multiple ways here, David, and every one of them is a jewel." David was surprised by Victor's response as he realized that this was the only time he had ever been with Victor without Katy present. He also realized that this was the only time he had ever been with Victor in any type of business setting.

As the conversation and wine were flowing and the food was being passed family style, Douglas Nickerson tapped his water glass with his knife. "First," he said, "I'd like to thank Victor for arranging this trip for us to learn more about Aclare and for providing what we all ascertain is going to be a wonderful dinner for eight hungry Minnesotans." There was a round of thanks and glasses raised to Victor. "Secondly, I know I said when we boarded the plane this morning that Melvin and I can't discuss any school business, at least just between the two of us, but I interpret the law not to inhibit two board members from participating in discussion with other informed citizens. So, let's make the most of what we've learned tonight to evaluate Aclare for St. Luke."

"If we go with Aclare, will Paul Simon play for the senior prom?" Bobbie teased.

"We'll make sure we get that in the contract," Ken Keegan laughed.

Victor spoke up. "Chairman Nickerson, with your invitation to make the most of the night to evaluate Aclare, would you please start our dinner conversation with your thoughts on what you saw this evening?"

Nickerson paused. "As chairman, I usually like to speak last, and as a Scandinavian I'm programmed not to speak much, and, with what little I say, to reveal even less. But at your invitation, Victor, I'll give my impressions without giving my opinion."

"Fair enough, Mr. Chairman. Lead us in discussion," retorted Victor.

"Well, first let me say from a pure style perspective, it was a damned enjoyable evening—good wine, great conversation, a provocative keynote, and world-class music. From a substantive perspective, if Taylor's claims prove out in his presentation next week, if the results he says he gets are data-based and hold up under scrutiny, there's more here than I thought.

Finally, I think St. Luke has several of the most interesting and controversial weeks ahead the district has ever seen. That doesn't mean I'm for or against Aclare. It just means this can't be dismissed out of hand. Taylor's not an opportunist or an interloper as someone called him at our meeting last week. Nonetheless, what he's proposing has widespread implications for St. Luke and for that matter the whole state of Minnesota. With that, I'll close my impressions and dig into this egg roll."

"I'll take your impressions, Doug, and raise them. Everything I heard at the reception and Taylor's speech point to a new day in American education," noted Monsignor Murphy. "Tell us, Victor, did you know of Aclare's China deal before tonight?"

"I had no idea about the international transactions, but over the time I've known Jack, he's shown me plenty of data that indicates Aclare gets great results. The news regarding China and South Africa took me by surprise. Jack mentioned in recent months that Aclare was preparing for some big announcements, but I took that to mean a contract with Los Angeles Unified or Miami-Dade County. I've got to tip my hat to him. He practices what he preaches. As Taylor said, the China deal exceeds by almost twenty times the number of U.S. students using Aclare. He tells America his product will help it compete in a global market, and tonight he showed the value the world puts on that product. Now if we can only see beyond our self-imposed limitations, we should take on Aclare."

"Who is *we*, Victor?" asked Melvin.

"*We* is St. Luke. *We* is Minnesota. *We* is America, Melvin."

"I couldn't disagree more. After what I've seen here in San Francisco," Melvin said, while moving his eyes between Sharon and David, "I say the man loves money more than he loves his country, and I for one cannot encourage St. Luke to do business with such a person. To think of selling his product to the Chinese . . . those cunning commies are stealing our jobs and trying to emulate our lifestyle."

Ken Keegan almost jumped out of his seat, "With all due respect to your position as board member, Melvin, are you out of your damned mind? First, some relatives of those cunning commies are currently serving us a sumptuous feast, and secondly, why in the hell shouldn't Taylor sell to

China? Regardless of whether we, America, want his product, if others do, more power to him. I don't buy his two reasons for a lack of market penetration in the U.S. I think it's bullshit, and he's just whining because it's tough, damn tough, to get shelf space in American education. He's just got to get his rear in line with hundreds of other vendors looking to improve American schools and, I might add, make a buck in the process."

"Amen," Bobbie added.

"I'll give the devil his due," Keegan continued. "If his product is as good as he says it is, bring it on. I've spent thirty years in public education. It needs an overhaul. But I want to see the end game. I refuse to be juked and jived by short-term objectives and improvement programs whose names we forget within two school years."

"Okay, Ken," agreed Melvin, "Taylor's just another in a long line of school-improvement vendors. But what sets him apart is his money-grubbing pandering to the Chinese. Anyone who would sell products or technology that helps the Asian horde move closer to our Western standard of living is no friend of mine. Further, his announcement this evening that a Chinese investment company now owns a significant portion of his company and holds a seat on his board sickens me. If we do business with Aclare, some of our school district's money will flow into the pockets of Chinese investors. That's un-American."          ·

"Honestly, Melvin, you're living in the past. The Cold War is over. Nixon opened China in '72. The Wall fell in 1991. Mao is dead. China is a crazy blend of communism and capitalism." Ken pushed back. "Why shouldn't Taylor improve the depth and speed of learning of Chinese kids? With one stroke of the pen he's reaching a quarter of a million students. Compare that to satisfying school board members like you, and union hostility, and tons of regulatory roadblocks like seat time, and inclusion, and title this and title that—all that bureaucratic crap that drags our schools down. The same guy that just signed up 250,000 Chinese kids is also working to land a deal to get a portion of the 300-kid St. Luke High School. That tells me this guy cares about America."

David was enjoying the parry and thrust between Ken and Melvin. He was rooting for Ken, who was arguing with his school board member boss just like he'd done dozens of times. David was suddenly glad Melvin was on the trip. In David's mind it was a no-lose proposition. If Melvin liked Aclare, Victor was one vote closer to success. If Melvin didn't like Aclare, which was probably Victor's expectation, no damage done. Melvin's opinion carried little weight. He argued over the smallest of points, protracted school board meeting after school board meeting, and continually alienated himself from his fellow board members and the community. For any person that Melvin might sway to his side, at least five others would take the opposite position. It was true on any issue. Melvin Vilsak was a pain in the ass, and David was delighted he was on the trip.

Turning his attention to Bobbie, Victor asked, "Bobbie, what did you think about this evening?"

Bobbie blew out a long breath. "While I enjoy a good time as much as anyone, that cocktail reception didn't seem much like a school event to me. I must admit, though, that seeing the association and the federation at the reception and learning that both organizations have money in Aclare sure surprised me. As for Taylor, I thought his speech was interminable and showed little understanding of American public schools."

"What do you think of Aclare's results?" Victor questioned.

"If teaching to the test is all our curriculum has become, then rote, computer instruction is cheaper and probably more efficient. But teaching takes many dimensions and computers can't replace people, at least not in schools. But, Victor," she leaned almost across the table and whispered, "While it's hard to dispute his data, I'm duty bound to oppose it."

Victor stretched to meet Bobbie and kissed her on the cheek. "I understand, and you're a treasure to our town."

Bobbie blushed. "Why thank you, Victor." Then looking over at David, she added with a grin, "I still think the old black woman was a plant," then sat back to enjoy the ongoing battle between Melvin and Ken.

David was engrossed in the fiery conversation. He was supercharged, famished, mentally overloaded, and enjoying himself. To his left, Victor was watching the show put on by Ken and Melvin, and every once in a while, he'd lean to his left and make a comment to Chairman Nickerson. To his right, David was surprised to hear words like political economy, neo-Marxism, and market protection from Sharon, who was fully engrossed in conversation with Monsignor Murphy. As David reached beyond Sharon for the wine bottle in front of Monsignor, his arm accidentally brushed her breast. Slowly, almost imperceptibly, her leg pushed against David's with a lightness, more pleasant than he would have expected, that left little doubt of its purpose. David mused at the irony of bonding with his father-in-law to his left while his intellectually engaging colleague to his right got flirtatious under the table.

Just before eleven, sated and exhausted, they left the Silk Dragon. There was little conversation as they enjoyed the quiet of almost empty sidewalks. David broke the silence when he asked Victor what they might expect at the shareholders' meeting tomorrow. "Nothing like tonight," Victor said. "When you get to your room, look over the agenda. It's routine and non-controversial as far as I can tell."

When David got back to his room, he didn't look over the agenda, but instead took off his shoes and shirt and brushed his teeth. Just as he was about to undress, there was a knock on his door. He was stunned to see Sharon there. "Hi, David, I wonder if I might use your bathroom." The request took David back. The toilet was clogged in her room was his first thought. He opened the door and said, "Sure."

Sharon closed the bathroom door behind her as David ran his fingers through his hair. "Uh, oh," he thought as he heard the bathtub being filled. Five minutes later Sharon came out wearing the hotel bathrobe. She pulled the covers down, dropped her robe, and got under the sheets. David didn't hesitate. He went directly to the bed and sat next to Sharon, looked in her eyes and said, "I hope I haven't misled you, but I won't do this. I could never break my vow to Katy. I've enjoyed the day and the dinner, but this would be wrong."

David couldn't read Sharon's expression. There seemed to be disappointment, relief, and rejection in her voice as she asked, "Who's to know?" and pulled the sheet away.

"We would," David said.

Sharon stood up, modestly pulled the robe around her, grabbed her things from the bathroom, and left.

# Chapter 9

# *Monday of the Sixth Week of Football Season*

THE LETTERMEN DID NOT HAVE A GAME the week David went to San Francisco. That was fortunate, for David had missed only two light days of practice. St. Luke's next opponent was Foley, one of the smaller schools in the conference and usually one of the easier games of the season. David had expected Carl to grumble when he told him he wanted to go to San Francisco for the Aclare meeting. Surprisingly, Carl didn't object and told David to have a great time and keep any eye on Bobbie. David felt it must have been the fact that St. Luke was on the downhill portion of an undefeated season that Carl had placed not even the slightest guilt on him for the trip.

David was glad to be back into the Monday night routine, watching tapes with Carl and telling him about the Aclare trip. Carl and David went right out to the boathouse when the Andersons arrived. The weather had remained unseasonably warm and the pan fish were biting. Bobbie fussed over Anna and seemed to treasure her role as a surrogate grandmother even more than usual. In fact, Bobbie was so enjoying Anna that Katy got things started in the kitchen. A half hour later Bobbie came in and said, "Anna's going to watch *Snow White*. I told her to call me when the witch comes on. You have a precious child, Katy. She is such a beautiful blend of you and David. Never forget what a gift you've been given."

"Thanks, Bobbie. I try to remember that every day. I wonder sometimes how it will be if we're fortunate enough to have more

61

children. How will Anna do, sharing our love and attention with a new baby, and how will David and I do with Anna no longer our sole focus?"

"Oh, Anna will do fine. She's made to be a big sister. Your devotion to her has provided her a wonderful base, and when the time comes she'll be as thrilled as you and David about another member of the family. I don't want to be nosy, but do you have any news?"

"Not yet, but we're officially trying."

Bobbie's eyes teared up, and she hugged Katy for a long moment, enough time for Katy to feel Bobbie sob and to smell the wine on her breath. Katy could see a half-empty bottle on the counter. Usually Bobbie waited for them to arrive before opening the wine. Katy thought little of it and enjoyed the extended hug and womanly tears of her dear friend.

"Oh, my goodness," Bobbie said as she relaxed her hug, "I must compose myself."

"Yeah, David and I think it's time to extend the clan. Boy or girl, it doesn't matter to us, but we joke that if it's a boy, Victor might kidnap him and raise him to be the heir to lead Gram Industries."

Bobbie smiled. "You might be right. Gram Industries needs a crown prince." Bobbie paused, then said, "Losing your mother was something I don't think your father has ever gotten over."

"Why do you say that?"

"Well, not that I follow your dad's social life, but he's never dated again, has he?"

"No, I don't believe he has. But that doesn't mean he hasn't gotten over Mom's death."

"Wouldn't he want to remarry to enjoy the companionship and love of a wife? He's got to be one of Minnesota's most eligible millionaires."

"I don't think Dad would ever see himself on such a list. I think that my mom and dad were so in love, so totally and completely the other's soul mate, that Dad has never even considered dating again."

"It's not like Victor would be looking to replace your mother; it's more like he might be interested in finding a new love, a new life. Heavens, how old is your dad, sixty-five?"

"He's sixty-four."

"Connie and Alfred both lived into their eighties, didn't they? Your dad could easily have twenty more years, and with his wealth, his mind, and his handsome grace, he might have nothing but enjoyment ahead of him."

"I don't think my father sees pleasure as a big part of his life. He sees his work as his life, and in the Benedictine tradition, he sees his work as his prayer."

"You know I'm a Lutheran, and Carl's a Methodist, and neither one of us is a good one of those. What do you mean by 'he sees work as prayer'?"

"In the Benedictine tradition, work is prayer and prayer is work."

"What?"

"Benedictine monasticism is based on creating a community of people who support one another in their search for God and in doing God's will. It's based on prayer and work. Whether a monk or sister is a baker or a teacher or an artist, nurse, accountant, farmer, the dedication to doing their best work is prayer. Likewise, prayer is work, the real work of the monastic. My dad became a Benedictine oblate after Mom's death and he tries to live within the Rule of Benedict."

"Wow, I'm a mature woman with two college degrees, but what you've just told me is something I've never heard of. No wonder Luther hung his Ninety-Five Theses on the door of the Wittenberg Church. The Catholic Church has so much detail, so many layers."

"You can say that again, Bobbie. Wanna sign up with the Benedictines?"

"No thanks. It's all I can do to make it to church on Christmas and Easter. Come on. We'd better get cooking or there'll be two ornery coaches, one Catholic and one non-practicing Methodist, in here in twenty minutes."

Katy and Bobbie scrambled to get supper on the table and finished just as the men walked in from the boathouse.

"Well, I think we'll do okay against Foley on Friday night," Carl said as he sat down.

"Carl, I'm shocked. We've been coaching together for years, and you've always sat down on Monday night expressing worry that our opponent is going to clean our clock. You going soft on me?"

"I just might be. I think I can see the end of the rainbow, so I need you to kick me in the ass and make sure we don't get tripped up in the home stretch."

"Gotcha, coach. I'm gonna ride your ass like you're a 200-pound freshman dough ball."

"Oh, boy, I'd better be careful what I ask for," Carl said.

Katy sat down, and Bobbie fussed even more than usual about the details of the meal. As she reached for napkins, she said, "David, we haven't talked since the trip to San Francisco."

"Well, a wrap-up of the Aclare meeting seems worthy of a dinner-time conversation," David replied. "And I didn't say much to Carl out in the boathouse."

"Sounds like it must have been a real adventure," Carl said with a mouth full of salad.

"I'd say it was. I'm sure you've heard most of the highlights already from Bobbie."

"Like the Paul Simon concert, and fabulous feast at the Chinese restaurant, and the luxury accommodations at the hotel?" questioned Carl.

"Well, yes, but beyond those highlights there was a lot of educational substance too," David said.

"I'll humor you, David," Carl grinned.

David hardly got a bite to eat as he told his tale of the details of the cocktail party and the people they'd met: the grandmother from Richmond, the investors, the union reps. Bobbie chimed in on Aclare's ownership by the unions. "Get a load of this, Carl. Both the major teachers' associations own stock."

"You mean the NTA and AFE own stock in Aclare?" Carl asked.

"What? Didn't Bobbie tell you already? That's exactly what we asked the two guys at the cocktail party, and they said the unions hold positions in a lot of companies they want to keep tabs on," David said.

"Why?"

"Having ownership gives the shareholder the right to attend the annual meetings, and have time with the board and management team."

"Interesting." Carl chewed for a moment. "So how many shares in Aclare do the teachers associations own?"

"I don't know, but I can say that the two union reps sure were taken by surprise by Jack Taylor's speech. They ran out of the room like their pants were on fire when he announced that an investment arm of the Chinese government was putting enough money into Aclare to get a seat on the board. But I'm getting ahead of myself."

David, holding a forkful of food poised between plate and mouth, told about the rally and the dinner at the Silk Dragon. Whenever Bobbie would add an embellishment or make a comment, he'd take a bite and then get back to the story.

Even though Carl and Katy knew Paul Simon had performed, they all enjoyed hearing about the pleasure Monsignor Murphy had had listening to the music and laughed again at the debate between Melvin and Ken.

As Bobbie described the South African kids dancing at the end of the rally to celebrate Aclare coming to their country, David finished his supper. Katy served everyone a large slice of apple pie with a scoop of ice cream. Carl was incredulous. "My God, Bobbie, I hope the insurance premiums are up to date. This piece of pie might be the death of me."

"Shut up, you old Bison, and enjoy it. If you croak, I'll bring an apple pie to your grave each year on this date."

"Ain't that romantic," Carl teased.

"What's your opinion of Aclare, David, now that you're one of the town's experts?" Carl asked. "I've heard Bobbie's view, and you can pretty much guess what she thinks."

Katy looked at David, who took a moment to wipe his mouth and gather his thoughts before he responded. While David had talked with Katy many times about the San Francisco trip, he hadn't come right out with his position on whether Aclare should come to St. Luke.

Carl's question was not hostile, but David knew this was a touchy issue. Carl was right. It was easy to know how Bobbie felt, and a disagreement on this subject would cut very close to the bone.

"Well, when we boarded Victor's plane to head to San Francisco, I wasn't sure what I was doing on the trip. But I'm glad I went. Despite, or in addition to, the fun parts, I found more educational issues to ponder and more challenging ideas than I anticipated. I even got a little one-on-one time with Jack Taylor. But three things really impressed me. First, the personal testimonials; Aclare has changed a lot of kids' lives."

"David, don't be so naïve. That Viola woman, for one, was a fake, and probably other Aclare supporters were as well," Bobbie blasted with more emotion than the comment needed.

"Hell, we all change kids' lives as teachers. That's what we do," Carl interjected, working to settle down his wife.

"Yeah, Carl, sure. But, Bobbie, what I saw was Aclare changing the lives of kids who'd previously had no hope. Not that you, me, Bobbie, and Katy don't help our students develop in a positive manner and, on occasion, keep a kid from making a major mistake. We all do that, and that's some of our best work. But what Aclare does that's different is that it reaches hundreds, thousands of kids in crappy schools with lousy teachers with a method that gives them content and knowledge that's not being effectively transmitted in far too many American schools."

"Baloney," fussed Bobbie.

"See, I told you it was easy to know what Bobbie thinks about Aclare," cracked Carl.

"The second thing that impressed me is tied to the first. Aclare's data on student performance is impressive. There's a ton of third-party research that shows its value. Broader knowledge, deeper understanding, and more rapid absorption is the way I boil it down."

"All computer-based instruction," added Bobbie, "no soft skills, no group projects, no relationship development, little interaction with the teacher, just machines passing content."

"I disagree, Bobbie. The program works so that one teacher can supervise seventy-five students. The program is content rich, very intuitive, and it drives higher order thinking skills, specifically synthesis and analysis. The students get engaged with each other and the instructor on topics and levels of thinking that go way beyond where they'd be in a traditional classroom."

David noticed that Bobbie's expression subtlety changed and she seemed to disengage from his description and focus on her own thoughts.

"The third impressive component for me was the way other countries are embracing Aclare. Just drawing from my comparative education class, I know that a good part of the world has nothing like we do in terms of our high school structure. Aclare offers those nations a cost-effective way to deliver schooling."

Bobbie got back into the conversation. "I see it quite differently from you, David. Regardless, do you think it has a place in St. Luke?"

David knew this was coming. He paused and shook his head. "I think it deserves an opportunity to have a pilot program. A pilot is reversible. If it doesn't work, it's gone. On the other hand, it might prove too valuable not to adopt."

Silence blanketed the room. Finally Carl blurted, "This Aclare thing can't coach football, can it?"

"No, dear, Aclare doesn't coach football."

"Good, then my job's secure."

"Hey," David said chuckling, relieved that the silence was broken. "I thought you were going out in a blaze of non-defeat in just a few weeks, Coach Tucker."

"Well, not if Foley cleans our clock this Friday," Carl said, working hard not to let the silence grow roots.

"Don't be so glib," snapped Bobbie. Silence returned until Bobbie let out a long sigh. "Sorry, Carl, I shouldn't have snapped at you. I've just got pressure on me from St. Paul. David, if you'd said Aclare has no place in St. Luke, my heart would have soared. But you gave your honest assessment, and it confirmed what I've been afraid of the last few weeks."

"What do you mean, Bobbie?" Katy asked.

"I mean that my friend, David, who saw what I saw, says Aclare is good. Now I've got a job to protect our teachers. St. Paul doesn't want Aclare to get a toehold in Minnesota."

David asked, "Does it have to be so black and white, a win-lose situation? Can't we have a risk-free Aclare trial?"

"I don't know. Maybe if we could contain it to St. Luke, yes, but we can't contain it. Everyone will be observing us if we do this, and St. Paul, specifically Bruce Barnes, has a 'kill the baby in the cradle' attitude toward this. He's even proposing legislation that will limit the amount of time a student can spend on computer based instruction."

"That's absurd," blurted David.

"That's the real world, David," Bobbie fired back. "I'd like to think I'm a moderate, not a radical, when it comes to my leadership of our local teachers association. We've had it pretty good in St. Luke, with minimal troubles."

"That's because the football team makes the community proud and happy," Carl observed.

"Carl," Bobbie said softly, "You're a great coach, and I agree that the Lettermen's success helps the community support the schools, but if Aclare comes, people will lose their jobs."

"But if Aclare doesn't come, Gram Industries will become less and less competitive, and people will lose their jobs, at least that's Victor's position," added Katy.

"Maybe it doesn't have to be so all or nothing," David said again. "We've got a fair number of teachers ready to retire. If Aclare works, perhaps it'll come in as teachers retire. The district won't hire new teachers but will expand Aclare."

"But you're not looking at the bigger picture, David," Bobbie said with an edge of frustration in her voice. "Even if it could work here, it means others will adopt it." Bobbie's voice quivered as she emphasized each word slowly, "And people will lose their jobs."

# Chapter 10

# Tuesday of the Sixth Week of Football Season

Everywhere he went, David was asked about San Francisco and Aclare. Everyone wanted his opinion: should the board allow the pilot project? David reiterated time after time his reasons: the testimonials, the convincing data, and the international demand. He hadn't realized when he went on the trip that he'd be asked for his views by so many people in the barbershop, at the gas station, on the sidewalk. He felt like a politician, open for anyone to ask his opinion.

He didn't hold back, and he didn't adjust his message for the asker. He realized quickly that his opinion was appreciated by some but disagreed with by many. He left the barbershop in an uproar one evening after practice. Joe Leering, who worked for Gram and whose brother was on the school board, asked David what he thought. The result was that two other patrons got into a shouting match over Aclare. David wasn't the target of the argument; he just ignited it.

The place where David felt the most dramatic shift in atmosphere was the teachers' workroom in the high school. Prior to Aclare, David was a loved colleague, a favorite teacher, even the nominee for Minnesota's Teacher of the Year. David wondered whether he would have been nominated if the Teacher of the Year selection committee had made its choice now rather than earlier in the fall. The camaraderie and bantering that used to characterize the teachers' room had been replaced with coolness toward David. At first he thought it was his imagination, but in the week between his return from San Francisco and Aclare's second appearance before the board, David went from big man on campus to persona-non-grata.

When Katy asked him if he was feeling isolated at school, David said he was getting a new perspective on friendship and laughed it off. Personally, he couldn't wait for the presentation at the school board meeting that night because he thought it would help those who were mad at him now to understand the value of Aclare.

The second board meeting drew an even larger crowd than the first. In small-town fashion people came early to get good seats. Some even brought sandwiches and drinks and ate supper in the board room in order to get the best view.

David got a seat in the back, and just after he sat down, Carl walked in and sat beside him. "What? You're not only attending the meeting, but you're early?" David teased.

"Hell, this is the best show in town tonight. I've got to keep current on this so I can start arguments in the barber shop."

The crowd kept coming. People were three deep along the walls, and both sets of double doors were opened to accommodate people standing in the hallway.

"Carl, do you think this turnout means support of or opposition to Aclare?"

"Well, I'm sure it's both, mixed with curiosity seekers and bored farmers looking for any excuse to come into town and, I might say, stop at the Dairy Queen on the way home. We'll see how it shapes up tonight. I know Bobbie's got a lot of pressure on her to keep this thing out of St. Luke. Hey," he added with a change of tone, "I hear you're getting some crap from our colleagues."

"Crap's a little too strong. I'd say it's more like the silent treatment. I'm hoping tonight's presentation changes some minds."

"That would be nice, David, but data won't trump jobs in this town. Taylor's program could make every kid a National Merit Scholar, but if it costs one association member's job, you can chuck it."

"I don't understand how Bobbie, an intelligent, independent woman, can be so locked into that kind of thinking," David said.

"Well, when she first engaged with the association, early in our careers, the teachers were really paid poorly and had no voice in their working conditions. I think her involvement over the years has really made things better for the St. Luke teachers. You're a bit young to appreciate what things were like when I was coaching here and you were still in Catholic grade school. That said, Bobbie knows every time she negotiated for a bigger piece of the pie—for better salaries—she was in essence negotiating against the students. This is a tough thing to say, a fine line Bobbie has walked, but, better salaries usually mean higher pupil-teacher ratios, less money for supplies and materials."

"But better salaries mean better, more dedicated teachers, teachers who don't have to hold a second job to make ends meet."

"Yeah, yeah, I hear you, but, there's only so much porridge in the pot and you've got to get your own without starving your neighbors. What worries me about this Aclare thing is how much pressure she's under from St. Paul to keep it out. That Bruce Barnes guy calls our house every night. I'm about ready to tell him to screw off."

Nickerson called the meeting to order. "Welcome back everyone; it looks like we've got even more here than two weeks ago. The room's mighty crowded, so I'll ask everyone to be on their best behavior. Please be courteous not only to our presenters tonight but also to those folks who didn't get a seat and are watching from the hallway. The order of business for the meeting has been modified so we can hear first from the folks from Aclare Learning. They have a thirty-minute presentation; then they'll take questions for an additional fifteen minutes. Afterward, we'll then conduct our usual business as fast as possible.

"As you know, last week eight of us from St. Luke went out to the Aclare shareholders' meeting. I'd like to publicly thank Victor Gram, who I don't believe is here tonight, for supplying the transportation and a wonderful dinner. The rest of the expenses were picked up by the school district. This evening's presentation is crucial. Today schools are data-driven. Every educational decision we make is supposed to be based on research. While that might be impractical at times, I don't think our guests from Aclare will have any shortage of data to share with us. Based upon what we learned in San Francisco, Aclare has been tested up one side and down the other. Our job tonight is to listen to the data they present and consider if it's right for St. Luke. That said, let's get started."

He paused, he added, "Mr. Taylor's not here tonight." A sigh of disappointment filled the room. David heard from the people around him, "I only came to see Taylor." "I missed him two weeks ago and people said he was great." "Screw Aclare if they don't send us their star."

"But," Nickerson added, "he sent three members of his corporation who've set up quite a program. The board and I will sit in those folding chairs over there so we can watch the presentation with you. The board had a few minutes to meet the Aclare representatives before the meeting started," he continued. "I'll let them introduce themselves. Ladies and gentleman, the floor is yours."

Where Jack Taylor had stood two weeks ago, two women and one man turned to face their audience. After introducing themselves, they said they would show a ten-minute video about Aclare and then move into the "dry" portion of their presentation—a PowerPoint on Aclare's results. The presentation would close with testimonials from parents and school officials after which they would take questions.

The presentation went just as it had been foretold. The video on Aclare included lots of waving American flags, happy faces, and kids staring at computer screens. David squirmed in his seat. The video was fluff. The data portion obsequiously pandered to high stakes tests and national standards, ran too long, and required too much concentration. Carl nodded off several times. How many of his colleagues stayed focused enough to follow it, David could only guess. He knew the average corn farmer phased out in the first two minutes and reengaged in the testimonials. The only problem with the testimonials was the urban and African-American focus. The presentations from teachers, students, and parents were sincere and moving, but not a single person wore a seed cap, or camouflage, or sounded like a Minnesotan. David's spirits sank. This presentation did not reach its audience.

72

The question-and-answer session was flat. No one attacked Aclare as money-grubbing pigs. No one asked how many teacher positions would be lost to Aclare. No one asked about profit margins, or international sales, or priorities, or control, or curricular alignment. Not one tough question was asked of the presenters. The Q and A was Minnesota-nice. David didn't feel embarrassed for St. Luke. He felt embarrassed for Aclare. All his hope for the program evaporated.

\* \* \*

KATY LISTENED AS DAVID DESCRIBED the presentation. She suggested that since David had been treated to the rally, anything short of that would seem flat and undersold. David agreed, but that didn't get him beyond the video testimonial portion of the presentation. True, David had been most moved in San Francisco by the African-American grandmother from Richmond. But the video shown to St. Luke was almost totally African-American, which David knew presented a cultural hurdle to the average person in St. Luke.

It was 10:30 by the time David had finished telling Katy about the meeting. When he had reached the end of his tale, seemingly out of nowhere, he declared, "I need to talk to Victor. The people at the meeting were devastated that Jack Taylor wasn't there. You could feel it in the air. Jack Taylor's got to be at the final meeting to get a favorable vote. Where's Victor?" asked David.

"I'm pretty sure he's in California," Katy said.

"Great, it's only 8:30 there. I'll call him."

Katy stepped back, "Hey," she popped, "did you and Victor get drunk in San Fran or do some male bonding or something?"

David stopped in his tracks, considered the question for a moment. "Yeah, I guess we did."

David talked to Victor for a half hour, analyzing the presentation by the marketing group and seeing it land flat on an audience who had come for some excitement, some yelling, some outbursts, Nickerson pounding his gavel, maybe even some pushing and shoving. But nothing of the sort had occurred. Everyone had behaved. Not a mind had changed.

"David, I'm glad you called. Not only is this critical information for Jack to hear, but also, you got me out of an incredibly boring dinner meeting. I was falling asleep. I'm going to call Jack. Thanks."

It was about 12:15; David and Katy had been in bed for half an hour when Victor called, "Katy," he said, "is David awake?"

"Sure, Dad."

"Hello," David said.

"David, I can tell you weren't awake like Katy said, but anyway, I talked to Jack. He said he'll come to St. Luke for the board vote if he can get five minutes to address the community. He said he wasn't surprised that the presentation fell flat tonight. He second guessed his choice of the team he sent, but in the final analysis it wasn't the people, it was the material, right?"

"Right, Victor."

"I got that message across to him. I'm surprised he's coming back to St. Luke. We're an ever-diminishing blip on his screen, and I don't understand why he's so committed to getting this district in his portfolio."

"Maybe he's just competitive enough to want to sign them all, big and small."

Katy hung up the phone and nudged closer to David. "I think Jack Taylor is going to come back to St. Luke," he said as he pulled her closer.

"Are you a Jack Taylor fan?" asked Katy.

"I'm an Aclare fan. It helps kids. As far as being a Jack Taylor fan, the jury's still out. I only spent a few minutes with him in San Francisco, and they were pretty generic. And, you know, I agree with Victor; something doesn't add up for Taylor to be so interested in St. Luke."

"Well," Katy said sleepily nestling on David's shoulder, "I imagine we'll find out Mr. Taylor's motivation soon enough."

# Chapter 11

# *Thursday of the Sixth Week of Football Season*

I[T HAD BEEN TWO MONTHS] since their neighbor, Linda Myers, had died, and David felt badly he hadn't visited Brooks in the interim. It was Thursday, about seven thirty. Katy and Anna were shopping. David didn't know if Professor Myers taught class on Thursday night, but the lights were on in the house, so David walked through the yard and around to the front door.

After ringing the bell twice, David was about to leave when he heard footsteps. Professor Myers opened the door, and, after a perplexed look, he recognized David with a huge smile, "David, David, my friend, my neighbor, my student, come in, come in." He grabbed David by the arm and ushered him into the house.

"I hope I'm not disturbing you."

"Disturbing me? There's nothing to disturb. I'm delighted to see you and in need of your company. Please, please come in, sit down, stay awhile."

David looked about the house. Everything was neat and clean. Although they had been neighbors for years, David had never entered the Myers' home through the front door. It made him feel more formal than usual. Until Linda's illness, she and Brooks had been great neighborhood walkers. Regardless of the weather one could see the two of them clipping a brisk pace, fully engaged in talking. It seemed they were always talking. David wondered how the professor was doing without his dear companion.

Most of the conversations David and Brooks had had were held in David's front yard. As he was doing yard work or playing with Anna, Brooks and Linda would walk by, and often Brooks and David would talk for a long time. Their areas of common interest included trees, shrubs, and grass, where Brooks was very knowledgeable and David often seeking advice; football, where David was the expert and Brooks the devoted fan; and education, where Brooks was the theorist and David the practitioner. The football and education talks had often led to a beer or a glass of wine on one of their three-season porches. The juxtaposition of their homes made them backdoor neighbors, and David enjoyed his friendship with Brooks, referring to him alternately as Professor or Brooks.

"Your home looks terrific, Brooks, inside and out," David said as they walked through the entry hall to the kitchen table.

"Thank you, David. Keeping it tidy helps fill the void right now. Sit down. I had just finished my supper dishes and was about to enjoy an after-dinner drink. Please join me."

"Thank you, I will."

Brooks set two Waterford roly-poly glasses on the table. Linda had loved Waterford crystal. The china cabinet was filled with Waterford glasses, and there were Waterford lamps throughout the house. The roly-poly was Linda's favorite for a cocktail because, as she had said many times, "It fits so nicely in the hand."

"These were Linda's favorites," David said.

"Ah, you remember, my friend."

"I want to say how sorry Katy and I are about Linda's passing; the neighborhood misses her presence. She kept us all connected somehow, with her walking."

"She kept me healthier with her walking. Without her, I would have sat on my rear end. She got me out, she made me more fit, yet she got ALS and was gone in a year."

"I'm sorry I haven't dropped by sooner. With football season, games, practices, Monday nights with Coach Tucker . . ."

"Say no more. It's good you didn't drop by earlier. I was a mess and so was this house. You would have thought I'd never pull myself back together after Linda's death if you had come by any sooner. The timing of your visit is perfect. I'm so glad to see you."

David got a lump in his throat in response to the candid and sincere welcome. "How are you doing?"

Brooks walked to the pantry, returned with a bottle of Glenlivet, poured David three fingers and himself two. "I don't know. I don't know. I'd like to tell you I'm fine and moving right through the grieving process, but I don't know. Linda and I were so close, so close." He shut his eyes as if to resist tears. "David, we were rarely apart in our forty-two years of marriage. We had an unusual togetherness, not just a physical presence together but an intellectual tie and spiritual unity that we both treasured. We even shared an office at the university, though we were in different departments...but you know that."

David smiled and nodded.

"I lost her and I lost half of me when she passed. Now the half of me that remains seems pathetically incomplete."

David didn't know what to say. Telling Brooks that he would get over it and things would be better soon was inappropriate. That would be a shallow response that put out the signal "stop telling me about your pain because I don't like to hear about unpleasant things." David just listened. That seemed his best gift to Brooks.

"You know, David, you and Katy have that same sense of togetherness. You're very fortunate. I think you both know it and cherish it. Never, never let it go or jeopardize it or risk it in any way. As a Catholic who hasn't been to Mass since the 1960s, I felt God's presence in Linda, and I saw heaven in our love."

Brooks took a sip of his scotch, and then there was silence, not uncomfortable silence, but reflective silence. Brooks finished his drink. "Now tell me about you, David, and Katy and Anna. Help bring me back to the world of the living."

While his mind had been made up to listen as long as Brooks needed him, David was excited to have a chance to talk about Aclare,

San Francisco, Jack Taylor, the unions, and the whole drama in town. He valued Brooks's opinion more than that of any of his other professors. Brooks had a wider vision and more experience as a professor than most of the faculty at the College of Education. It wasn't just his age that separated him from his professional peers; it was the route he had taken to gain his wisdom, his perspective.

"But before we talk more, let's move to my study. The chairs are more comfortable there."

Indeed they were. Brooks had two deep-cushioned armchairs, in addition to his desk and desk chair, in a beautiful study. David had never been in the study before, and it seemed exactly as it should be, cluttered but clean, oozing books and thoughts, comfortable yet productive. Brooks sat in the far chair, flanked by two pictures. One was of Linda and Brooks in some type of protest march, the only two white faces in a crowd of black people; the other picture was of Linda in profile with a fiery sunset behind her. She had been a beautiful woman.

"Now tell me, David, catch me up, what's going on with your family and what about this Aclare thing? Since I'm on leave from the university, I'm out of touch. Help me catch up. I think that's a good sign, don't you?"

"It certainly is a good sign," David smiled as he worked on his scotch. He hadn't realized that Brooks was on leave and felt even worse that he had not visited him since Linda had died.

Brooks poured himself another scotch and added more to David's still unfinished glass. He settled comfortably back in his chair in anticipation of letting David talk.

After a quick catch-up on Katy and Anna, David started the Aclare saga. Brooks was an active listener, probing, asking for clarifications yet letting David keep the story rolling. He understood Victor's desire to get smarter workers, but was suspicious of Taylor. What was his background? What did he know about schooling? About teaching? About learning? He asked about the teachers association and Bobbie Tucker, and found union ownership of Aclare a twist he'd never imagined. He inquired as to where his former student, Superintendent Ken Keegan, was on Aclare, guessing that he'd support it but would avoid stating a position until necessary. He laughed at Keegan's exchange with Melvin Vilsak at the Silk Dragon and said that was the best laugh he'd had in months. Brooks listened intently and sipped his third glass of scotch as David finished the tale.

"Well done, David. It's a great story. You've not only caught me up, but you've entertained me mightily. But where," Brooks stumbled with his words, the first sign that the scotch was affecting him beyond lifting his spirits, " ...do you stand on Aclare?"

David had known Brooks would ask. "Well, Professor . . ." David paused and collected his thoughts. "When I first heard about Aclare, I immediately felt we had no need for it in St. Luke. We were doing just fine here. I think that's how nearly everyone in St. Luke felt. Then I went to San Francisco and saw what Aclare has done. No, we don't need Aclare; we're doing okay, but with Aclare we could do so much better, and I, as a teacher, want the best for my students. I'm in favor of Aclare coming to St. Luke."

David studied Brooks's face. The professor looked tired. "Well stated, my boy," he said without changing his expression. David knew the Myers to have always been on the leading edge of education issues and always focused on social justice. He understood that Aclare's approach represented a radical departure from the government-directed tinkering that's usually involved in school improvement efforts.

Brooks poured himself one more finger of scotch. David passed on another round. "This will be my last of the evening, David. I've had far too much Glenlivet, but it was a wonderful accompaniment to your story."

David agreed and waited, as it was clear Brooks had something to say.

"I met Linda in graduate school at Columbia in 1966. We were two Minnesota kids lucky enough to find themselves at an Ivy League school on the cusp of a social upheaval we thought would change the world...or at least America. The ink had scarcely dried on our dissertations when we moved to Charlotte, as researchers to study the court-ordered desegregation of that district. We were jubilant, in retrospect; tendentious, but jubilant, ready to use our newly minted doctorates to empirically demonstrate that bussing for racial balance would lead to better schools.

"Oh my, what a snake pit we found ourselves in. Bussing didn't work. Bussing tore communities apart. And after five years, Linda and I moved on. Our experience in Charlotte put us close to professors of education all over North Carolina. Of all places, we most enjoyed the people at Appalachian State, way up in the mountains in Boone. We both took assistant professorships there and dug into improving some of the worst, most impoverished, Third World schools in the mountains. We really loved Boone. But our parents got old and sick. My only sibling, an older brother, died in Vietnam. Linda was an only child. So we looked to move our careers back home.

"We got here in our prime, both of us in our mid-forties. We accepted tenured associate professorships. Shortly after arriving in St. Luke, the tenor of education began to change. Kennedy's New Frontier, Johnson's Great Society, even Carter's banal optimism, these noble social ideals began to come under attack. For Linda and me, education was the way to improve society, and public schools provided the education for ninety percent of America's kids. Our lives as education professors, our work to uplift the poor and disenfranchised came under attack, not an attack on us personally, but an attack on education as an equalizer, as a way to improve society.

"The change began with the election of President Ronald Reagan. He was cynical about government. He changed the dialog about public schooling. Prior to Reagan, schools were for kids. Adults made the rules, but the rules were for kids. Reagan started the painful situation we continue in today.

"*A Nation at Risk*, that warning that we were losing in the international education race, started it all. It was never talked about, but we were losing in the international race based on totally different expectations than those that guided American schools. Other nations haven't peacefully desegregated their society through their schools. Most nations don't spend tens of billions of dollars a year on educating those with handicaps. It might not make economic sense, but it's damn good for the kids it serves and the right thing to do.

"While America attempts to educate every student regardless of ability, potential, or attitude, we're compared to nations that track kids to vocational work, weed out the average, and focus on the cream of the crop. *A Nation at Risk* put our children's development at even greater risk. Adults still make the rules, but they don't make them for children anymore. They make them for politicians. Teachers don't work to meet the needs of their students anymore. They work to prepare their children for tests. We've changed, David, from a child-centered system to a test-centered system."

Brooks was emotional. This was a cathartic moment. In two minutes he'd summed up over forty years of work in public schools. David could see the emotion, the letting go brought on by the death of Linda, the discussion, and the scotch. Brooks paused. David wondered if he was finished, if he might pass out. Brooks sighed and tears welled.

"David, something ineluctable must happen. Perhaps Aclare is the next step. The center cannot hold. What Aclare and its brethren, charter school companies and online learning companies, represent is the future. There's no doubt about it. Mind you, it's no universal benison to the nation; market forces have their Achilles' heels." Brooks was slurring his words badly now. "I'm a liberal, David, and proud of it. Fifteen years ago I would have lain down in front of a bus to stop private companies from getting a piece of public schooling. But public schooling took on the mantle of being market-oriented itself by making programs to satisfy a growing consumer market. We made post-secondary enrollment options for kids to go to college while yet in high school. Does that make sense? Just let them go to college. We created open enrollment and let parents choose where they wanted their kids to attend. We made magnet schools and single-gender schools, charter schools, all in response to market needs. Yet when free enterprise knocks on the door of public education, it finds hostility and suspicion. Why? Because the system fears competition. Because public schools have a crazy sacrosanct position in the American psyche. Because schools are no longer about kids; they're about money and jobs."

Brooks slowed. "David, it may come as a great surprise, but, after this little outburst, lecture, if you will, I want Aclare to come to St. Luke. Schools reflect the societies they serve, and despite my distaste for consumerism, Aclare reflects this nation." He was slowing down even more, beginning to fall asleep. "David, my generation had its shot at improving schools. We had a few great victories, but we didn't win the war. This Aclare is worth a try. Everything has a life, you, me, Linda. Aclare too. It and its kind won't live forever, but with each generation we take ideas and build upon 'what is' to make 'what will be.'"

Brooks closed his eyes once more. David wondered if that was the end of his moving synopsis of his life and vision of the future. Then Brooks's eyes reopened. "David, your visit has meant the world to me. I am better for it!" He said groggy and half-asleep, "May God bless you," and then closed his eyes.

David looked at Brooks, beginning to snore. He took a quilt from the back of the chair and wrapped it around his neighbor. He put the Glenlivet back in the pantry, washed the Waterford, turned out the lights, and locked the door on his way out.

# Chapter 12

# *Monday of the Seventh Week of Football Season*

IT WAS A SPECTACULAR LATE OCTOBER MONDAY. The air was clear, clean, and crisp. Most of the leaves were off the trees, yet the grass was still green and St. Luke looked neatly manicured as David drove to work. The Lettermen had enjoyed two easy games on the downhill side of the season. Carl was planning to announce his retirement on Friday night, after an away game and the next to last of the regular season. The final game of the season at home against Brainerd would be a tribute to Coach Tucker and an inspiration for the team to perform at peak level in the state playoffs.

David felt wonderful after the win over Foley. He'd had a restful weekend of yard work, watching football, and a nice bike ride with Katy and Anna. The only disappointment of the weekend was that he hadn't gotten to the hardware store to purchase the long list of items for his projects at home. He'd tucked $150 in his wallet, but the weather had been just too perfect to spend time shopping.

Fifteen minutes into his first-period class, the P.A. system crackled. David was called to the office. "Excuse me, class, I'll be back in a moment." Having to take care of something in the office was routine, but it usually didn't involve being pulled out of class. Sue Rogers, the plump and jovial school secretary, one of David's favorite people in the building, shrugged her shoulders as he walked into the office. "Mildred Townson wants to see you," she said.

*Mildred Townson,* David thought. *The school business officer? What would she want to see me about?*

David entered her office and was surprised to see Melvin Vilsak standing behind Mildred. "Good morning, Mildred. I'm surprised to see you here, Melvin. What's up?" There was an awkward silence.

Mildred hesitated, then said, "David, school board member Vilsak has a concern regarding your trip to San Francisco."

"What kind of concern?" David asked, even more puzzled.

"I'm sure it's just a simple misunderstanding that can be cleared . . ."

Melvin interrupted Mildred's efforts to look on the bright side. "David, we received a bill from the Pacific Pass Hotel yesterday. The school district paid for our hotel rooms, you might recall."

"Sure, I remember."

"Your room had $125.80 charged to it for a bathrobe," Melvin said in an accusing tone.

"There must be some mistake," David responded. "I didn't take the bathrobe. I don't even wear a robe at home, but that's probably more than you need to know." Then it hit him; Sharon Lunsford had walked out of his room wearing the bathrobe. He couldn't say, "If housekeeping would check the record, I'm sure they found two robes in Sharon's room." No, he couldn't say that. He couldn't say the truth.

"Look, if there's been a mistake, I'll pay for the robe, which I don't have. I don't want the school district to pay for it."

"But, David," Melvin sneered, "you said you don't have the robe. You didn't take the robe."

"That's right."

"Then why would you pay for it?"

David froze. The reason he would pay for the robe was to clear the books, get the robe off the school district's record and not let a silly bathrobe create an ugly scene. He suddenly realized that Melvin wasn't looking for the $125.80 to reimburse the district; he was looking for something beyond that. David remembered Melvin looking through the window as he caught Sharon after she had slipped by the pool. And Melvin had rounded the hallway corner as he and Sharon came out of her room on the way to the Aclare reception. David's stomach knotted as he realized what conclusion the prurient-minded Melvin had reached.

Quickly assessing the situation, he thought several plays ahead. David would cut Melvin off at the knees. "My mistake. This is a mere imbroglio, Melvin, " he said in a cold and calculated fashion, looking straight at Melvin. "I did take the robe and forgot to pay for it on check out." Changing his tone back to his friendly self, David looked at Mildred. "Mildred, let me take care of this little problem right now so Mr. Vilsak will be able to rest comfortably as a steward of the school district." He pulled out his wallet and placed $125 on Mildred's desk, then reached into his front pocket and added eighty cents. Melvin fidgeted and puffed like a toy train. "There, I believe this ends the matter of the bathrobe."

"Yes, David, that will be . . ."

Melvin cut Mildred off again. "I don't think it's going to be that easy to clean up this misunderstanding, as you call it, Mr. Anderson."

David felt satisfied he had flustered the dimwitted Vilsak, yet he was infuriated as he walked back to his classroom. Melvin thought he'd screwed Sharon in San Francisco. Beyond being a tight-ass, busybody who would love this type of bedroom gossip any day, Melvin now would do his best to embarrass David, his wife, and father-in-law in an effort to keep Aclare out of St. Luke.

Two doorways from his classroom David spun on his heels and headed to the science wing. He hadn't seen Sharon since they had returned from San Francisco. He wasn't sure what he was going to say to her, but her behavior was no longer a mere social miscalculation; it was now a threat to David's reputation and his family. When he got to Sharon's classroom, the smell of formaldehyde met him as did a short woman with gray hair. "May I help you?" she asked.

"Yes, I'm looking for Ms. Lunsford."

"I don't know where you'll find Ms. Lunsford. I'm Ruth Jordan. I was called last night to be a substitute. My husband and I just retired here last month. He loves to fish, especially ice fish, and I'm a certified science teacher. It has worked out wonderfully for us. These students are so well behaved. I don't wish the regular teacher any harm, but I hope this assignment lasts awhile. I'm just so—"

"Thanks anyway,"David said, then walked out the door. He went to the office, bent over Sue Rogers' desk, and whispered, "Sue, I need a few minutes to make a call, please get someone to watch my class."

Sue put her hand over David's. "Sure, I'll take care of it. Everything's going to be all right."

"Do you have a list of faculty phone numbers?" Sue, handed him the faculty directory, and David copied Sharon's home and cell numbers. He went to his car and called Sharon's home number. No answer. He tried her cell.

"Hello, this is Sharon."

"Sharon, David Anderson."

"Oh, hi, David. How are you?" she said pleasantly.

"I've been better. Where are you?"

"I'm in St. Paul. I just parked near the association office. I was asked to attend a meeting here, so I took a professional day."

"I'm sorry to trouble you, but I thought you should know this. A few minutes ago, Melvin Vilsak called me into the office and accused me of taking a bathrobe from the Pacific Pass Hotel. There was an invoice for $125 charged to my room for that robe."

"Oh, my goodness. What did you say?"

"Well, I couldn't tell Melvin that the robe from my room wound up in your room."

"Thanks. I appreciate that."

"After initially saying that there must be some mistake, I changed course and said I had taken the robe. I just happened to have enough money in my wallet to pay for it right then and there."

"Oh, David, I'm so sorry. I owe you $125 and a gigantic apology. I'm so impressed with the way you handled the situation in your hotel room. Katy is one lucky woman. I ask your forgiveness for my inappropriate behavior, and I'm sorry I haven't apologized to you in person."

"Sharon, I'm not looking for an apology."

"But, David, I so enjoyed getting to know you in San Francisco. I think the combination of our swim together, the exhilaration of the rally and dinner conversation, mixed with a liberal amount of wine resulted in me making a rather bad and embarrassing move. Please forgive me."

Sharon's apology was so sincere David was almost speechless. He feebly said, "Okay, apology accepted." Groping for something to change the conversation, he asked, "What are you doing at the association office?"

"I probably shouldn't say this, but I'm meeting with Bruce Barnes, and I have a feeling . . ." she paused. "I think he may offer me a job."

"Wow," David heard himself say. "But you already have a job."

"That's true, but Barnes asked me to meet with him here in St. Paul. He said there were some things he'd like me to do for him."

David scrambled for words, not understanding what Barnes could want Sharon for. "Good luck," was the best he could produce.

"Thanks, David. And I'll send you a check for the robe right away."

David went back to his class. The conversation with Sharon stayed on his mind all day. The distraction was so great that he sent a message to Carl that he'd be late for practice and went home right after school.

When he arrived , Katy was just coming out with Anna in her stroller. Katy called, "What's wrong? Why aren't you at practice?"

David hadn't thought through what to say to Katy. He was kicking himself for not having told her the entire Sharon fiasco right after he returned from San Francisco. Still, he hadn't done anything wrong. "I need to talk to you."

"Shall we go in the house, or can we talk while we stroll Anna?"

"Let's walk. It's beautiful. Maybe the fresh air'll clear my mind."

"You handle pressure like nobody I know. You can have a 300-pound gorilla trying to cream you and still get the pass off. So what's significant enough to rattle you?"

"Right now I wish I had a linebacker bearing down on me. That's easier to take than the current garbage."

"What do you mean?"

"Well, there was a strange twist of events today."

Again Katy asked, "What do you mean?"

As they strolled Anna, David told Katy the Sharon tale—the swimming pool, coming out of her room with Melvin walking by, her under-the-table flirtations at the Silk Dragon, and the coup de gras, Sharon getting into David's bed in the buff.

"And what did you do at that moment?" Katy asked.

David told her and was never so thankful for uncommitted sins.

"Okay, Sharon got aggressive, made a major league pass at you, including getting between the sheets in her birthday suit. That's a pretty clear indicator that a girl's willing. And you, good husband and father that you are, sent her packing in a hotel bathrobe. I love it! I love you. But why didn't you tell me about Sharon's antics before?"

Sheepishly David reminded Katy of how loving she was on his return and that he didn't want to spoil the moment by telling her Sharon had tried to bag him in Frisco.

Katy laughed and hugged David. "You knucklehead. You put good communication behind good sex?"

"Guilty, a thousand times guilty, but I never saw, never thought, Sharon's stupid behavior would end up getting Melvin's attention. It was so meaningless that I just didn't bring it up."

"But you didn't have sex with her, David."

"That's right, but Melvin thinks I did."

"What?"

David told her about Melvin's inquisition about the bathrobe, adding that Melvin had seen him holding Sharon after she slipped at the pool. He told Katy that he was worried Melvin would use the rumor to embarrass him and the Grams and play up the San Francisco trip as a love junket to discredit Aclare. David added, "I'm hard pressed to see how a missing bathrobe means a sexual encounter, but I'm not Melvin, and his mind operates on a strange plane. So I told him I have the robe and paid Mildred $125.80 right in front of Melvin with the cash I'd planned to use at the hardware."

Looking puzzled, Katy asked, "Why'd you do that?"

"Because I couldn't tell him the robe was in Sharon's room, and by paying for it, I neutralized some of the evidence Melvin is using to try to embarrass me."

"Wow, is there anything else?"

"Oh, yeah," David drew out the words. "Sharon's not at school today. I called her. She was very understanding and apologetic. She said she'd pay for the robe and begged me to forgive her indiscretion. But, get a load of this, when I reached her on her cell, she was sitting in front of the association office in St. Paul about to meet with Bruce Barnes. She said she thought he was going to offer her a job."

"This doesn't add up. Something smells fishy," Katy said. As they were rounding the corner heading back to their house, they saw Victor's car parked behind David's and Victor sitting on the front porch. He got up when he saw them and met them on the sidewalk.

"I figured when I saw David's car home early that you were talking about the thing I came here to discuss."

"Sharon Lunsford?"

"Yes. Katy, I came here to make sure you were all right and to stand up for David, just in case he needed it," Victor added with a grin. "But I can see my skills were not needed to avoid marital discord."

"No, Dad, I know all about Sharon Lunsford. David came home to tell me the strange twists that occurred today. But how did you know?"

"About an hour ago, my secretary put a call through to me saying, 'I have a caller who won't identify himself but says he has an important message for you.' I took the call and a male voice said, 'Your son-in-law screwed Sharon Lunsford in San Francisco. Thought you'd like to know.'"

"Dad, what the hell's going on?" Katy piped.

Over coffee in the kitchen, David told Victor the Sharon story. He had never imagined that he would be telling such a tale to his father-in-law and in front of Katy. Victor listened to David's story, peppered with Katy's remarks, plus the tales of Melvin's bathrobe inquiry and Sharon's absence. "It seems Aclare has stirred up some of the less desirable qualities in at least one of our board members," David noted.

"Do you think Melvin called you?" Katy asked her father.

"I'm not sure."

Katy left to attend to Anna as Victor prepared to get back to his office. "David, can you walk me to my car? I've got a few more questions."

Victor got in his car and lowered the window. "How well did you know Sharon before the trip, David?"

"Hardly at all."

"David, when you told Sharon no, what happened?"

David paused, "Victor, she pulled back the sheets and revealed her damned good-looking body. I thought she was just drunk and doing something she'd regret in the morning. I knew I'd regret it. What bothers me most is that Melvin has drawn his own conclusion."

"Look, David, if my instincts are right, the association was working to entrap you, embarrass the two of us, and get me to pull back on Aclare. Melvin's just a small-minded Puritan who's now an unwitting accomplice in the association's plan. What concerns me most, David, is not the potential for small-town gossip. You, Katy, and I know the truth. If rumors fly, we can't let them hurt us. No, what concerns me most is if Bobbie Tucker knew what was going on. I can't imagine she had anything to do with it, but if she did, it would be devastating to Katy."

# Chapter 13

# *Monday of the Seventh Week of Football Season*

DavID STOOD IN THE DRIVEWAY and watched Victor's car turn the corner out of sight. He observed how such a beautiful morning had turned cloudy. Inside the house Katy asked if he was going to return to practice. "Yeah, I'll head back in a bit, but I think I'll do a little raking first." He paused. "We do need to head to the Tuckers' in a couple of hours to watch tapes with Carl."

With a weary look, Katy said, "Okay." Katy Gram Anderson had grown up surrounded by a constant discussion of high-level deals, confidential agreements, and intelligence gatherings. Her instincts were leading her to the same question Victor had about Sharon's purpose on the trip.

David stepped out to re-rake the yard. It was still nearly leafless from his weekend work, but being outside gave Katy some space she seemed to need.

When he went back in the house, Katy said, "David, you know what I think?"

"What's that, honey?"

"I think Sharon Lunsford was sent on that trip to bag you."

David waited a moment. He knew his next sentence would confirm Katy's instincts. There would be negative consequences. Slowly he offered, "That's what Victor thinks."

"Damn, damn, damn." Katy's eyes filled with tears. "Do you think Bobbie knew this?"

"I don't think so, Katy. No, let me be clear. Bobbie had nothing to do with this."

"If Dad thinks Sharon was on that trip to compromise you and the Gram family, it makes it rock solid in my mind. Gram Industries might be in small-town Minnesota, but for three generations we've dealt with the seamy side of the business world—people offering under-the-table deals, kickbacks, bribes. My father knows what he's talking about."

"Damn that bathrobe. I should have sent Sharon back to her own room in her birthday suit."

"It's not the robe, David. Even if the hotel hadn't charged for the robe, the rumor would still have been started. The robe just fed Melvin's suspicious mind. Now that idiot will do all the dirty work, and the association can just sit back and laugh."

"But still, Katy, Bobbie didn't set this up."

"But, damn it, she didn't stop it either," Katy shouted. "How could she allow them to rip at the fabric of our family?"

"Katy, how could she stop it if she didn't know about it?" David whispered as he wrapped her in a hug.

\* \* \*

IT WAS CLEAR TO EVERY PLAYER on the team from the look on David's face that to give anything less than 110 percent would result in disaster. David went through what remained of practice with intense concentration, as if the Brainerd Warriors were the Wisconsin Badgers. He ran his players ragged, not out of anger, but out of confusion and frustration.

He loved football, yet he didn't want to follow Carl as head coach. For David football was no longer the center of his life, and he knew in order to be a successful head coach, football had to be the focus. The events of the past weeks turned over and over in his mind as he put his players through their paces: Bobbie's immediate worry when she heard the name Jack Taylor, Carl's speech on football as the glue that holds schools together, Aclare's rally and his glimpse of what education might become—high performance yet soulless. Then there was Melvin and Ken's argument over the future of schooling, Melvin's bathrobe accusation, and Victor's anonymous caller. He could feel his blood pressure rise as he thought about Sharon. If she was indeed on a mission in San Francisco, who was to know she'd failed to accomplish her objective? Who would be callous enough to put his reputation, but more importantly, Katy's feelings, in jeopardy?

He blew his whistle and watched forty teenage boys drag themselves to the locker room. He felt like he had just conducted his last practice. He knew he would struggle to put his heart into football again. He knew that meant he couldn't take the head coaching role, but he didn't know how and when to tell Carl. He didn't want to overreact to the situation, but it wasn't just the Sharon thing. His head hurt as he walked off the practice field. Carl passed him in the locker room. "See you at six thirty?"

"You betcha," David replied flatly.

* * *

IT WAS A TENSE DRIVE to the Tuckers' that Monday night. Silent. Katy was distracted. David knew she was connecting the dots, rejecting any notion that Bobbie had a hand in the Sharon Lunsford affair, but angry that Bobbie was tied closely to those who did.

When they walked into the Tuckers', the table was set, but there was no Bobbie. "Strange," David noted, "sure is quiet. Carl's probably in the boathouse."

Just as David was heading out the back door, Bobbie yelled from the back of the house, "Katy, David, is that you?"

"We're here, Bobbie," Katy responded. "Everything okay?"

Bobbie emerged from the hallway. "Oh, yeah, I just decided to put a bit of myself into the meal." She held up a bandaged left index finger. "Oops."

"Are you all right?" Katy whispered as she laid a sleeping Anna in the crib Bobbie and Carl kept for her in the family room.

"I'm fine. Just annoyed with myself for not paying attention. Come on, let's get supper rolling."

David murmured, "I'll just head out to the boathouse." But before he reached the boathouse, he sensed that things were not all right and turned around and reentered the house just as Bobbie was saying, "Katy, I can't believe Victor got such a call."

Katy looked up at David. "We both feel needlessly maligned," he offered.

"David, I thought you were out in the boathouse," said Bobbie.

"Thought I'd offer to help out here since you're working with a handicap."

"I'm doing all right. I've still got nine working digits."

Katy asked, "Bobbie, why did you select Sharon Lunsford for the San Francisco trip?"

Bobbie continued to shred lettuce. "I didn't have anything to do with that."

"What?" Katy asked glancing over to David.

"What do you mean, Bobbie?" David asked.

"I was lucky to have gone myself," Bobbie said, "Sharon Lunsford was Bruce Barnes' choice."

"What? Why in the hell does Bruce Barnes get a vote?" Katy asked.

"Because, damn it, Katy, Bruce Barnes is my boss in the association. That's why. He thinks I'm too close to you and the Gram family to be objective, and that my caring for you makes me soft on keeping those bastards out of here."

"Screw Bruce Barnes. If he doesn't like our relationship, that's his problem."

Katy rarely lost her composure, and David was taken aback to see Bobbie and her arguing. He was glad he wasn't out in the boathouse. "Look, let's calm down and take the situation apart piece by piece."

Katy would have no part in deescalating. She was a mother bear. Her instincts were rock solid. She had just witnessed the hack job perpetrated on her marriage and sensed the goons who had set it up. She wanted an explanation. "Why did Barnes send Sharon to San Francisco?"

"I don't know."

"Bobbie, you're lying to yourself. My husband's good name and our marriage are being attacked. Other people may take infidelity or out-of-town affairs casually, but I sure as hell don't. Tell me why Sharon, who is no senior member of the faculty, someone modestly engaged with the local association, was chosen by Barnes?"

"When I learned he'd chosen Sharon, I was puzzled. When I saw her on the airplane, I was dumbfounded. When I heard what you just said about the anonymous call to Victor, I was sickened."

"Did you know she wasn't at school today?" asked David.

"Yes."

"Do you know where she was?"

"No."

"I spoke to her. She was parked outside the association's office in St. Paul. She said she'd been asked to attend a meeting."

Bobbie stopped shredding lettuce, paused, then spoke slowly, "Who asked her to attend a meeting?"

"Barnes," David replied.

"I don't get it," Bobbie said.

"I think you get it, Bobbie," Katy said, "I just think you don't want to admit it."

"Get what? Admit what?" Bobbie snapped.

"Bobbie," David asked, "did you notice anything peculiar about Sharon's behavior at the restaurant in Chinatown?"

"Well, not really."

"Bobbie, she sat between you and me."

"Well, she seemed quite engaged in the conversation and perhaps had a bit too much wine."

Katy was pacing. David had never seen her so coiled. Bobbie was swinging between irritable and confused, argumentative and defensive. David knew he had to tell Bobbie the whole tale, but Katy beat him to it.

"Bobbie, Sharon Lunsford was sent on the trip to screw David."

"I don't believe that," Bobbie said, putting her hands on her hips.

David stepped in. "Bobbie, after the dinner at the Silk Dragon, I went to my room and was brushing my teeth when Sharon knocked on my door and asked it she could use my bathroom. So I let her in. She went into the bathroom, took a quick bath, came out in the hotel bathrobe, walked to the bed, dropped the robe, and got under the sheets."

Bobbie thought for a moment. "David, you're a good-looking guy. She drank a lot of wine at the dinner. She made a mistake."

"That's what I thought, a stupid indiscretion, when I asked her to leave."

"Did she leave?"

"Yes. She picked up her clothes and left my room wearing the hotel bathrobe. I thought that was the end of it. I didn't even tell Katy about it until today because I thought it was meaningless, but this morning Melvin called me to the office, accusing me of taking a robe from the Pacific Pass. The school district got a bill from the hotel, charged to my room, for the bathrobe."

"What did you do?"

"I couldn't very well tell him that the robe in question was in Sharon's room, so I paid for the robe, right there in front of Melvin and Mildred Townson."

"Do you think Melvin called Victor?"

"I don't know, Bobbie, but when I reached Sharon this morning, she was outside the association headquarters. She said she was meeting with Barnes and thought he was going to offer her a job."

"What!"

"Don't deny it, Bobbie," Katy pushed. "Sharon was picked by Barnes to get dirt on David and try to get Victor to back down on Aclare."

"Oh, that can't be. The association doesn't work that way. It doesn't have sleeper units across America, buttoned-up science teachers it unleashes as sex bombs for strategic purposes. I may not like Barnes, but I'm damn proud of the association."

"Maybe this isn't business as usual for the association, but this sleazy action sure happened in this case. I don't think you had anything to do with this, Bobbie, but the association doesn't play within the lines. Are you going to resign and expose this vicious game?"

Bobbie looked stunned. "Well, Katy," Bobbie fumbled, "it's just not that easy."

"Being right isn't always easy."

"You don't understand. You just don't understand," Bobbie railed. "The association does good things. It brought teachers fully into society, gave us decent wages, protected our working interests, ended favoritism, fought unfair dismissals. It increased our benefits, united our voices. Without the association, teachers would still be chattel. You're too young to know how things were, Katy."

Katy stepped back from Bobbie's heat. "The solution has become the problem."

Bobbie's face flushed. Before she could respond, the phone rang. She took a deep breath, composed herself, and answered. "Hello . . . Ken . . . no I was unaware of that . . . yes, I'm quite surprised." Bobbie placed herself in the corner of the counter space, faced away from Katy and David, and lowered her head. "This is unexpected and unprofessional. Thank you for letting me know so quickly, Ken. Good-bye."

Bobbie stood motionless a moment, then turned around. "Sharon Lunsford resigned this afternoon effective immediately, for personal reasons." She stood still several more seconds, then began to tremble. "Damn Aclare. Damn Sharon Lunsford," she screamed. She picked up the large yellow salad bowl filled with the bounty of her love, raised it above her head and smashed it against the kitchen floor. "And God damn Bruce Barnes."

Anna started screaming. Katy picked her up and held her tightly. David stood in disbelief. Carl walked through the back door and froze. Hand on the door knob, he surveyed the wreckage and said, "Holy shit."

Chapter 14

# Tuesday of the Seventh Week of Football Season

K<small>EN</small> K<small>EEGAN</small> <small>WALKED OFF</small> the eighteenth green at the Northern Pines Golf Club. He was pleased to have the chance to get another round in before winter. Whether this would be the last of the year, he didn't know, but he was glad he had left his office at three o'clock to walk the back nine alone on this Tuesday afternoon.

Ken Keegan was a dedicated public school leader. He had grown up just outside of Elk River, some fifty miles northwest of downtown Minneapolis. His family had raised potatoes and corn on two sections of land since his great-great-grandfather and great-great-uncle had homesteaded in the 1870s. By the time he was fifteen, Ken was certain of one thing. He didn't want to be a farmer. He set his sights on higher education and became the first member of his family to receive a college degree, a B.S. in social studies education from St. Cloud State University.

He enjoyed teaching but saw the limits on his salary. In his quest for improvement, he completed his administration degree at the University of Minnesota. Evening classes for four years kept him away from his wife and children several nights a week, but his intelligence and dedication impressed his professors. Hard work was what Ken did best. His Ed.D. degree opened doors to him at an early age. He had earned his stripes to take the leadership at St. Luke. While it was by no means one of the larger districts in central Minnesota, its football heritage and strong local funding made it a sought-after position.

His tenure had been characterized by solid community support, two successful levies, improved test scores, amicable teacher negotiations, and stable enrollment—a small town miracle. He had a good situation in St. Luke. Nickerson managed the board well, ran a good meeting and kept things under control. Melvin Vilsak was a pain in the ass, but what school board didn't have its troublesome characters? He could work with the other board members. He had even perversely grown to enjoy arguing with Vilsak. Early in their relationship, Ken had decided he wouldn't hold his tongue. If St. Luke didn't want him and Vilsak tried to fire him, he was confident he would find any number of good superintendent positions, a better option than biting his tongue and kowtowing to an imbecile. Everyone in town understood who the alpha male was in that relationship. Everyone, that is, except Melvin.

This round of golf had given Ken time to let his subconscious work on Aclare Learning. Over the last weeks Ken had certainly drawn the attention of his peers. Right after the San Francisco trip, he had held an impromptu question-and-answer session at the Central Minnesota Superintendents' weekly luncheon. He had received at least two dozen calls from peers and board members around the state. Those calls had ranged from "Keep the bastards out" to "Leadership calls for taking risks." It was time for him to make his decision. While he didn't have a vote on the matter, the board would ask his opinion, which would be taken seriously and would likely influence undecided members.

Keegan broke the Aclare question into three parts: student achievement, teacher issues, and the ongoing state revenue shortfall. The first issue was a slam dunk in favor of Aclare. He had been impressed with what he had learned in San Francisco. Since then he had read everything he could get his hands on about Aclare, and he'd had lengthy conversations with two associate superintendents where Aclare was operating. Despite the animosity Aclare had stirred up in those districts, its academic results were solid and incontrovertible. Yet Keegan understood the frailties of classroom instruction. He knew there was nothing more glorious than an effective teacher, but he also knew that all teachers weren't effective. He took to heart in the Olympic motto "Faster, Higher, Stronger." If Aclare could give the students of St. Luke a deeper knowledge base and a better capacity at critical thinking, he was all for it.

The teacher issue was more difficult. Good relations between teachers and the school board made a tremendous difference in any school district. Keegan understood that St. Luke would go from good teacher relations to strained teacher relations in one board vote should Aclare be approved. He attributed the excellent relations with the St. Luke Teachers Association to Bobbie Tucker. He saw her as mature, level-headed, community-minded, and realistic. Her leadership was superb. She neutralized the radicals and refused to defend the incompetents, much to the displeasure of the state office in St. Paul. But Keegan knew St. Paul wouldn't let Bobbie Tucker have full rein on the Aclare issue.

He too had been surprised when Sharon Lunsford had been chosen to represent the association in San Francisco and stunned by her transformed appearance on the trip. Yesterday, Ken had spent most of the day at a conference in St. Cloud. He had returned to his office just minutes before Sharon came in, unscheduled, and resigned. He had been baffled by her resignation, but the pieces fell into place shortly when Melvin had barged into his office to demand that David Anderson be reprimanded for his behavior in San Francisco. Ken had relished telling Melvin, "You prove to me they had sex or you shut your damn mouth for the good of the district. Besides, why just discipline David? Melvin, you're a troglodyte. You're just trying to create a stink that'll discredit Aclare or Victor Gram's support of Aclare. You could get the district in a load of trouble. So shut the hell up. Besides, Ms. Lunsford resigned less than an hour ago."

Ken knew Bobbie Tucker would never have orchestrated such a crass move as sending Sharon on the trip. He knew Bruce Barnes was behind it all and that reason alone was enough to throw his weight behind Aclare. On the whole, he supported a clean, clinical trial period. He felt it was not just about St. Luke, but offered results that would have bearing on the entire state and thousands of small districts across the country. If supporting Aclare cost him his job, so be it. His conscience was his guide, and it was pointing him to take a risk for the potential benefit of the students. Few things had changed as little as public schooling in his lifetime. He wasn't one to hold on to the current ways for fear of change. He knew that either decision would gain him fans and foes, but he was too old to care and too young for it to be fatal.

Besides, Ken knew that the Aclare trial had to take place, not just for St. Luke but for the whole state. Ken was in his second year of a three-year term on the advisory board for the State Superintendent of Schools. In the past two quarterly meetings of the advisory board, a picture had formed that sent shudders down Ken's spine. The state was seriously behind in revenue collection. The spending frenzy that had driven the economy of Minnesota and the rest of the nation had dried up almost overnight. Banks had failed. The government had intervened in Wall Street mishaps. People, for the first time in Ken's life, were scared. Scared for the economy. Scared for their jobs. Scared for the future. Ken was unsettled by the speed of the transition from go-go economy to one of mistrust and fear. He knew the ramifications for public schools—reduced state support, increased pupil-teacher ratios, reductions in workforce. He also knew that the Aclare model, if it worked, could ameliorate much of the pain for school districts that he saw coming. This third factor sealed the deal in his mind. He would support a pilot for Aclare.

\* \* \*

AS KEN WAS ENJOYING A COLD BEER at the clubhouse, Monsignor Murphy was pulling into the long driveway of the Gram mansion. Monsignor parked in front, got out of the car, then reached back in to pick up something from the front seat. As he closed the car door, he placed a black book and purple stole in the pocket of his top coat. This routine was a familiar pleasure to him. For years dinner at Victor's home was a regular occurrence. It wasn't always on the same day of the week or even the same week of the month, but it kept to a schedule of every four to five weeks.

Victor's cook, Harriet, prepared a dinner over which the men discussed politics, books, church events, and local news. They retired from the table to Victor's study for spiritual direction. Monsignor had been trained some twenty years earlier by the Jesuits in Omaha, and he served as the spiritual director for the diocese's seminarians and young priests, as well as handful of parishioners including Victor. At the end of the discussion and reconciliation, it also brought the pleasure of a fine cigar and a generous glass of port. The wine and smoke were pure pleasure, sometimes taken in silence and at other times with a return to the news of the day.

"When Anna died twenty years ago, my prayer life changed."

"That was a painful time for you, Victor, but one of spiritual growth. The death of a spouse, especially in the prime of life, drives many away from God."

"Monsignor, I had my anger. I cursed God. I was beyond hope. I stopped praying. I didn't care. Without Anna I was rudderless. I even stupidly sent Katherine to boarding school."

"Old wounds, Victor. Why do you bring them up tonight?"

"Because, as you know, when I began to pray again, it was 180° different than it had been. Until Anna died, I petitioned God, laid out my list of wants and needs and traded good behavior in exchange for God's blessings."

"And despite your petitions, your prayer, and your good behavior, Anna still died."

"Yes, and for a long time I felt prayer was worthless and self-delusional. Eventually, when prayer came back to me, I found myself a listener rather than a talker. The petitioning, controlling prayer, my list of needs and worries, was gone, replaced by a prayer of awareness and an attempt to see God in others and in my every action."

"'Be still and know that I am God.' That's mature prayer, the prayer of old monks and truly holy people, often people protected from the pushes and temptations of the world. Rarely is it the prayer of someone fully engaged in commerce and worldly matters."

"But I've regressed."

"What do you mean?"

"Of late, I've have been praying for victory."

"Victory?"

"Yes, a school board victory. A vote for Aclare."

"Why do you say you've regressed?"

"Because I'm asking God to grant my desired outcome. Not His will be done, but my will be done."

"Aren't you being a little hard on yourself, Victor? By no means is petitioning sinful."

"Agreed. But lately it's been harder to listen and easier to talk, to ask, to make sure God gets my request loud and clear."

"Even the holy ones who are the astute listeners still have their days of angst and doubt."

There was a pause. "Do you think God cares about the future of Gram Industries?"

"I don't know, Victor."

"Does the Church care?"

"Do you mean our little parish, St. Ansgar, or the Holy Roman Catholic Church?"

"The big one. Our little parish is behind me 51 to 49," Victor joked.

"Well, the Church doesn't care."

"Why not?"

"Because the future of Gram Industries is not a salvation matter. The Church is concerned with salvation issues."

"But the Church cares for its people: for workers, for widows, and children."

"For married people and wealthy industrialists too, Victor."

"Yes, but didn't John Paul II embrace capitalism after the fall of the Soviet Union?"

"I think *embrace* is too strong a word. For most of the twentieth century, the Church balanced itself between the despotism and oppressive nature of socialism and the greed and degradation of runaway capitalism."

"Yes, but now that socialism has collapsed in the USSR and remains alive only in isolated countries like Cuba and North Korea, isn't the Church ready to side with the free markets?"

"Victor, you've read *Centesimus Annus*?"

"In the early 1990s, yes. But please refresh me."

For the next half hour, Monsignor Murphy led Victor through over a century of Catholic thought on capitalism. Beginning with Pope Leo XIII and his encyclical, *Rerum Novarum* (*The Condition of Labor*), he ended with John Paul's *Centesimus Annus*. Written in 1991 by Pope John

Paul II, it denounced the inhumane exploitation that can occur in the name of capitalism, but it nonetheless expressed that market economies offered the best hope for the developing world.

"So," said Victor, "the Church does care about my business!"

"You have done, Victor, what people on both the right and the left have done with *Centesimus Annus*. They see it supporting their position. Part of the genius of John Paul was his capacity to see many perspectives and, thus, lead a diverse flock in more or less a single direction."

Victor said, "I'm pleased the Church cares for Gram Industries."

"I yield, my friend. As your spiritual director, I'm happy you feel supported by Rome and will not dispute the comfort you find in one of John Paul's most important letters."

"Nevertheless, I feel guilty about using one of my capitalistic tools."

"How is that, Victor?"

"You know Joe Leering?"

"Not well. He attends the other parish. But I know his brother, school board member Tom Leering."

"Well, you are with me then, Monsignor. Joe has worked for me for about twenty years. He's good and steady, very dependable, but reached his peak years ago at Gram Industries."

"I don't follow you."

"I called Joe into my office and let him know that, if he could make sure his brother votes for Aclare, I'd send Joe and his wife to France to represent Gram at an international conference and provide them with ten thousand dollars spending money."

"Victor, that's not like you to bribe an employee. That's an abuse of your role."

"I know. And I ask forgiveness for this and for another breach in my relationship with God. I have recently kept company with a woman."

"Victor, this is an area the Church certainly frowns upon, but it's common. I add with some reservation, an understandable transgression."

The men sat in silence for fifteen minutes. Monsignor granted absolution. Victor said, "Are you ready for a cigar?"

"Indeed I am," replied Monsignor as he took off his purple stole.

# Chapter 15

# *Tuesday of the Eighth Week of Football Season*

T HE SHARON LUNSFORD RUMOR never got legs in St. Luke. It passed like a brief autumn rain shower, forgotten within days. Her absence meant nothing to the community. The real winner in her resignation was Ruth Jordan, the certified science teacher whose husband retired to St. Luke to fish.

The town buzzed about Aclare in the days leading to the school board vote. St. Luke's *Leader* offered extensive coverage on the subject. It ran stories from newspapers in cities where Aclare was operating, as well as from *Education Week*. It did its own original reporting and conducted interviews with school officials and parents from several East Coast cities. However, its journalistic coup was an interview with Jack Taylor, complete with a head shot Aclare supplied after Taylor conducted the phone interview from his home in San Francisco. *The Leader's* story was divided almost equally between Taylor's personal history, Aclare's results in other districts, and what Taylor hoped to accomplish in such a small district as St. Luke. There was no mention of Aclare's announced business in China or South Africa.

The articles in *The Leader* fueled local discussion. Despite the fervor of debate around town, it was difficult to say how the vote would go. There were no polling services taking the pulse of the community. The school board had the final say, and in typical fashion the board members, with the exception of Melvin Vilsak, were not expressing their positions.

In the final issue before the deciding school board meeting, *The Leader* ran an interview with Ken Keegan. In advance of the interview, Keegan spoke with each board member. He didn't want a board member learning of his position in the newspaper. His first call was to Chairman Douglas Nickerson. Nickerson was pleased that *The Leader* was interviewing Keegan. "Ken, your opinion is important. It's good to get it out a few days before the board vote. What are you going to say to the paper?"

Ken described his three-pronged analysis to Nickerson—academic results, teacher relations, and state revenue challenges. Nickerson didn't say anything immediately when Ken said he supported an Aclare pilot project. After a more-than-awkward moment, Chairman Nickerson said, "Ken, I know you gave this a great deal of thought. The district is lucky to have you. If the pilot is approved next week, our relationship with the teachers will change. I'm not concerned about our local people, but the folks in St. Paul are going to create trouble."

"I hear you, Doug. But I can't let the threat of trouble prevent us from giving this a try. That's my position."

Ken's call with Vilsak was fun. He waited to phone him in the evening after dinner. Ken knew Melvin would attack him, so he was ready for the conversation. He called Melvin from his den with ESPN on the television, a beer in his hand, and a supply of cashews at the ready. Melvin didn't disappoint. Ken enjoyed the call, even when Melvin said, "You know this could very well mean your job."

The rest of the calls went quickly. All the board members thanked Ken for his advance notice of the upcoming interview. Some asked a few questions on his support of the Aclare pilot, but no one indicated how he or she would vote. Ken hung up from his final call comfortable with his communications. He had made his position and rationale clear. He was the professional, the life-long educator stating his position to his elected school board members. Regardless of the outcome of the vote, he felt he was on solid ground. He could lose his job, but his professionalism and his integrity were intact.

Those same two qualities also served Bobbie Tucker as the board vote to Aclare drew closer. She too had spoken with each board member, some several times. She had expressed her opposition to an Aclare pilot project and her fear that the pilot was merely a Trojan horse, Aclare's way of getting into the district and never leaving. She cited Aclare's history around the country of expanding programs within school districts despite strong opposition from the teachers.

The board members didn't perceive in their many talks with Bobbie the extent of the pressure she was receiving from Bruce Barnes. They knew Barnes mostly from the evening newscasts from the Twin Cities. Over the years he had had great exposure from teacher negotiations and strikes. He was articulate, mature, ruggedly handsome, and passionate in his defense of teachers. The association represented about seventy percent of the teachers in Minnesota public schools, so his opinion was often sought by the media, and, thus, he was a frequent guest on radio and television talk shows.

Bruce Barnes was an interesting operator with a complex personality. He had been elected to the top post of the association twelve years before and had remained virtually unchallenged. He was a master of the media and gifted in public relations and organization. For years he had organized the association to build houses for Habitat for Humanity. Each June immediately after school was out, they built four three-bedroom homes in various parts of Minnesota in a single week, paying for every nail and square foot of carpeting with donations from its members. It was far more than a publicity move; it was an organizational masterpiece that showed the association's commitment to the less fortunate. It was Barnes's idea, and his personality and administrative skills made it a perennial winner for the association.

The association was committed to assist the indigent, homeless, and new immigrants, and it was consistently the state's top provider of groceries to the food shelves, blankets and goods to the homeless. With Barnes center stage, the association truly had a heart, passion, and mission for those working their way up in America. As a result of his leadership skills, he was frequently considered for a national post with the association. He was clever and compassionate, but combative.

Barnes rubbed many in his organization the wrong way. Beneath his polished exterior ran a hardcore union man. He'd grown up in the coal fields of western Pennsylvania. His father had been a miner and then an organizer of the United Mine Workers. He was versed in hard-ball labor practices and used them when necessary. Among teachers in Minnesota, Barnes was consistently praised for results but frequently criticized for his tactics. His retort to critics was succinct: "I deliver."

A widower, Barnes was frequently seen at Twin Cities functions with an array of beautiful and not infrequently famous women on his arm. Bobbie's indignation toward him was understandable. She was the association's elected leader in St. Luke, responsible for good salaries for the teachers and positive relations with the school board. Bruce Barnes's interference could only harm the local community. The only strings she had to play were the ones she relied upon during her many years as local association head: good relationships with the school board members, honest communication, and a true sense of community spirit.

Over the years Bobbie had won many issues by this upfront community-focused approach. It wasn't her style to ask board members how they would vote on an issue. Rather she made her case and awaited the outcome. Vote counting seemed a waste of time. She was often amused by the composition of the vote but usually not surprised by the outcome. So when she got few signals on how people would vote on Aclare, she wasn't concerned. But that didn't satisfy Bruce Barnes, who wanted a nose count. He didn't like surprises. He wanted to know the results *before* the vote. This left Bobbie unnerved.

She worked hard to contain her aggravation with Bruce and managed to limit his involvement in St. Luke to daily phone calls to her home. She knew if she showed her emotions or dodged his calls he would show up at school and change the balance of power in the district. She listened and cajoled him into staying out of St. Luke. Barnes did stay away but told Bobbie, "If you lose the vote next week, I'm stepping in immediately, and I mean immediately."

\* \* \*

DAVID HAD CALLED JACK TAYLOR and opined that Jack's presence was critical to a yes vote. Convinced that the spontaneous bond he had formed with the community on his initial visit was real, David felt it wasn't enough to guarantee approval. "Jack, this community feels like it's insignificant in the Aclare world," David offered. "If you want St. Luke as a way to show Aclare's value to small-town America, this is your chance. Show up for the board meeting, preferably alone again. It'll make a big impact."

Taylor said he would look at his schedule and see what he could do. Later he called Ken Keegan to see if he could get on the agenda. Keegan told Taylor that he was certainly entitled to attend the meeting but that the period for public comment would be closed and voting on the matter would be the focus of the meeting.

Taylor called Victor. "David thinks my presence would be helpful in getting a positive board vote. It would let St. Luke know that it's significant."

"I concur."

"You've got a smart son-in-law."

"Indeed."

"Do you have a sense of how the board will vote?"

"I'm sensing a favorable outcome, Jack, but I also believe there are several members who're still on the fence. Your coming could favorably affect their votes. I'm sure your presence won't negatively affect the outcome. Put another way, your odds are increased if you come, with no greater downside risk."

"Sounds good, Victor. I'll make my arrangements."

"If you're in town early enough, let's have supper at my house before the board meeting."

"Will you attend the meeting?"

"No, I have to be in New York by noon the next day, so I'll be in bed by ten for an early rise. Besides, I think the Aclare vote is scheduled pretty late in the meeting, so there's no point in getting there before 9:00 p.m. or so."

"Thanks, Victor. I'll call your assistant with my arrival time. Since the meeting will run late, I'll need to stay the evening. Got a suggestion?"

"I recommend the Nightfall. It's nice. It's local. And it's wired."

\* \* \*

ON THE AFTERNOON OF THE BOARD MEETING, Taylor flew into Minneapolis, rented a car, and arrived at Victor's at six o'clock. Victor had asked Monsignor to join them for dinner. After a cocktail, the three men moved to the dining room. Monsignor asked, "Jack, how do you see Aclare fitting in with your Catholic faith?"

"That, Monsignor Murphy, is a question I've been waiting five years for someone to ask me."

"Really?"

"So help me God," Jack grinned.

"Then we're all ears," said Victor.

"First, what is this wonderfully presented meal we are about to eat, Cornish hens?"

"Pheasant, my good man, harvested earlier this week by me and my hunting party just west of St. Luke."

"Pheasant? This will be my first."

"This is our first of the season and let's not allow it to be your last," Victor said raising his glass in a toast.

"Welcome to the northern prairie," added Monsignor, "but back to the question you've wanted to answer for five years."

"Well, are you familiar with *Centesimus Annus*, Pope John Paul's encyclical from 1991?"

"Yes," Victor noted. "It's funny you should mention it. The Monsignor and I discussed it just last week."

"You're pulling my leg," Taylor replied.

"No, we're as serious as Leo XIII was when he wrote . . ."

"*Rerum Novarum,*" all three men said simultaneously.

Taylor paused, looked at his dinner companions, and said, "*Centesimus* saw me through the wild ride of the '90s and encouraged me to exit the investment banking business and refocus my business skill on a socially relevant enterprise. My goodness, you know what I'm talking about."

Victor and Monsignor were well into their pheasant by the time Jack took his first bite. "Hey, this is delicious," he crowed as he gobbled down several forkfuls. "Well, since you know *Centesimus Annus,* you must understand the tie between Aclare and my faith life."

"I believe I do," said Victor, "but you might need to explain it further to our local representative of the Church of Rome."

"What Victor is saying, Jack, is that he and I see *Centesimus* from different perspectives, and my guess is that yours is very aligned to Victor's."

"I see the encyclical as a statement of support for using free enterprise to raise all boats—the poor, the disenfranchised, women—"

"And public school students?" Victor asked.

"Exactly, my friend."

"Monsignor, do you not see *Centesimus Annus* in a similar way?"

"Yes and no, Jack. Yes, in that you should find encouragement for Aclare in *Centesimus.* No, in that it isn't a wholesale endorsement of capitalism."

"Funny to hear that from an Irishman whose countrymen have ridden the Celtic Tiger, a living example of creating opportunity and development in what just twenty years ago was the backwater of Europe."

"Point taken, Jack. Nonetheless, I have many friends, perhaps more to the left of present company."

"Hey, hey, hey, Monsignor, don't call me a righty," Jack said laughing.

"Thank you, Jack. For over ten years, I have tried to convince Monsignor that just because I wear a tie everyday, own a prosperous albeit small company, and live in the lap of luxury, I am not a righty. I'm a socially responsible capitalist. That is my secular humanist title. My Catholic title is *Centesimus Annus* capitalist." Victor winked at Jack.

"Hear, hear, Victor," Jack added, and for the entire dinner, Jack and Victor peppered Monsignor with their enthusiasm for capitalism as the agent for lifting the common man.

Monsignor warned that *Centesimus* railed against the greed of capitalism. "As a Catholic priest, I caution that those who use *Centesimus* as theological coverage, as moral salve to reap excessive profits, do so at their own spiritual peril."

"But that's not us," said Jack. "We're the good kind of capitalists. We improve the lives of children and families. We make our money from improving inefficiencies and increasing quality."

"My good man, you and Victor both rush to what you feel is the ending point of *Centesimus* without considering its many truths. You find your justification and ignore everything else about the encyclical. *Centesimus* is a long and thoughtful journey, but you skip, pole vault, helicopter to the end and avoid the full thought process. The result is a bridge that spans the chasm but bears no weight. That, I fear, is a metaphor for America."

"What do you mean?" Jack asked.

"You noted that Ireland was a backwater country until recently, and I cannot disagree, at least not regarding its economy. But what Ireland lacked in economic well-being before the rise of the Celtic Tiger, it made up for in community. When I left home, a newly minted priest, I was thrilled to come to America. For 120 years prior to my arrival the Irish had flocked to the shores of this wonderful nation. The America that I found on my arrival has drifted in many ways that are harmful. One major change is the dominant culture of consumerism manifested here and exported around the world.

"Indeed Aclare improves the learning of children and is more efficient and effective with taxpayers' money, but it does little to address the ethical and community dimensions America thirsts for. Aclare comes dangerously close to the commoditization of education, scoring high on productivity but low on relationship. Education is more than a consumer product. America must measure itself by standards other than production and consumption."

"But, Monsignor," retorted Jack, "on the basis on input and output, our public schools are a disaster. Five hundred billion dollars spent for a sky-high dropout rate and mediocre test scores. Waste, no accountability, and bureaucracies beyond belief."

"Yes, there are wastes and inefficiencies," Monsignor said. "Every organization—schools, churches, hospitals, manufacturers," Monsignor nodded to Victor, "have waste and inefficiencies. These are human organizations, fraught with the imperfections, inadequacies, and shortcomings of human beings. I don't defend waste, even if America's bounty leaves tremendous room for it. But even bureaucracies have a positive side. They employ people and give them purpose and stability."

"Spoken like a true Irishman, where being on the dole is a full-time job."

Monsignor laughed heartily, then composed himself. "Aclare's efficiencies place less capital in people. As a result, you have more profit. You spread that wealth around to your investors, and, if you grant a dividend, your shareholders. Public education spreads that wealth around to its teachers and administrators. Same amount of money, it's a zero-sum game, kept in the national economy yet spread through the local economy in different ways. *Centesimus* doesn't decry your profits, nor does it cheer them."

Jack wiped his mouth, placed his napkin on the table and asked, "Then what does it do?"

"John Paul wrote *Centesimus* for the world, but I think America was his focus. This nation's economic system must retool itself for justice. It must care about its communities, not from a public relations perspective, but from a human perspective. It must act as a nation as Gram Industries does in its local concern."

Victor raised his eyebrows.

"What is it that you do, Victor?" Jack asked earnestly.

"I'll answer that for him, Jack. He cares, and his legacy is not about himself but about those who work for him.

"When I arrived in America, I learned a lesson as I was driven to my first parish assignment eight hours north of Mobile, Alabama. It was July. I was miserably hot in the nun-chauffeured car. But before that day was out, I learned—and have never stopped appreciating—how big America is. Aclare has a place in this county's future. But to give it a chance to take root, to have its season, you've got to stop seeing the present structure of schooling as an enemy, stop kicking it in the shins. Befriend it in understanding and respect for the wonderful way it has served this nation. Waste and inefficiency, bureaucracy and failure are the background noise of our economy. Like the cicadas I heard my first day in Alabama, their sound dominated the environment. Embrace the people, Jack, as well as the process."

"Very good, Monsignor," Jack conceded. "There's more to discuss, but you have the final word this evening. It's almost nine, and I must go to the board meeting. I don't want to just slide in right before the Aclare vote."

\* \* \*

WHEN TAYLOR ARRIVED AT THE MEETING, the parking lot was nearly full. A brisk wind whipped him as the first Alberta Clipper of the season raced through central Minnesota with strong winds and the promise of a dusting of snow.

Jack entered the boardroom through the main doors at the rear. He saw a single empty seat on the end of the first row. As he walked to it, a murmur ran through the crowd. He heard his name whispered a dozen times. He also heard: "He came," and "He does care." He took his seat, and being as unobtrusive as possible looked around for David. He didn't see him but was delighted to see Katy off to his left. She nodded and smiled.

Jack had not arrived too late. He got to see the end of "New Business," which was the recognition of twin sisters, Nell and Dell Odegaard, for twenty years of serving food in the high school cafeteria. There were numerous food jokes and wisecracks offered from the audience and the board members before the sisters were given a weekend trip to Minneapolis, including tickets to see the Vikings play the San Francisco 49ers. Under "Old Business" he heard the final report on the condition of the bus fleet, listened as the board heard the ranking of bids to tar the roofs on the high school and elementary school gyms, and endured a preliminary committee report on Title 1 Part A compliance.

It was ten o'clock before Aclare came up for a vote. Douglas Nickerson spoke. "I don't think we've ever had three school board meetings in a row so well attended as we have these past three. The Aclare pilot has certainly gotten the attention of the community, and from my perspective that's good. St. Luke is a public school district, and it takes the public to make it operate. Regardless of whether you are for or against the Aclare pilot project, you have been immersed in education talk for weeks here in St. Luke. The types of discussion I've overheard in coffee shops and at the grocery store, I believe, have raised the level of analysis the average citizen around here gives a school issue, and that's good.

"I see Jack Taylor made the meeting," Nickerson said. Jack grabbed the recognition, stood up, nodded to Nickerson, and then turned and nodded to the crowd. There was a smattering of applause and a lesser mumble of boos. "Well, it seems," Nickerson noted, "that at least a few folks are glad to see you."

"Thank you, Chairman Nickerson," Jack said then added, "and you and you and you," as he pointed in the directions from which the applause had come. That drew a chuckle. Turning back to Nickerson, he said, "I am pleased to be here. St. Luke is very important to me and to Aclare Learning." He sat down, having gotten his message across without even being on the agenda.

"Then that brings us to the Aclare vote. Discussion has taken place at the last two board meetings. We heard the report from the delegation we sent to the Aclare meeting in San Francisco. We have each done our own research on Aclare and have heard the opinions of many community members. We know that Superintendent Ken Keegan favors the pilot. We know that association President Bobbie Tucker opposes it. Now it's time to find out how the board feels. Do I have a motion to move to a vote?"

"So moved," piped in Melvin Vilsak.

"A second?"

"Second," said Tom Leering.

"As customary, we'll do a voice vote followed by a roll call vote if needed. Mrs. Bolton, please read the question we're about to vote on."

Aggie Bolton, the recorder, stood and read the measure. "The school board will vote whether to establish a pilot program with Aclare Learning to be operated within St. Luke High School during the second semester of the current school year. Financial terms have been agreed upon by Aclare Learning and the St. Luke School District. The performance terms for the pilot must be met in order for the district to consider extending the agreement beyond the pilot program. The performance agreement calls for a composite increase in the scores of those students participating in the pilot program of greater than or equal to twenty percent beyond their composite scores on the Minnesota Academic Assessment Test from one year earlier. The test will be administered in late April. A vote of yes from a board member signifies approval of the pilot program. A vote of no signifies disapproval of the pilot program."

"The motion has been made," Nickerson stated, "and seconded. The measure has been read. Are the board members ready to vote?" Heads nodded affirmative. Jack Taylor looked to his left. Katy was looking at him and slowly winked her support. "Then I call the vote," said Chairman Nickerson. "All in favor of the Aclare pilot say aye, those opposed say nay."

A predominantly aye vote was clear to the entire assembly. Nickerson seized the moment to avoid personal rancor. "It is a clear vote in favor of approving the pilot program with Aclare. The measure passes."

Eight board members were ready to move to other business, but Melvin was restless in his seat. "Mr. Chairman," he said, "I request a roll call vote."

Chairman Nickerson tersely replied, "Melvin, we all heard a voice vote in favor of Aclare."

"I am not so certain, Mr. Chairman, and by Roberts Rules of—"

"Yes, Melvin, we all respect your mastery of the rules of procedure. I called for a voice vote because I felt it best served the district's needs. Had it been a nay vote, I dare say we would already be on to our next item of business."

"I contend it indeed may have been a nay vote and formally request a roll call."

Nickerson steamed. Melvin had the right to request a roll call, but everyone in the room heard a 7 to 2, maybe a 6 to 3 voice vote in favor of Aclare. Having a roll call needlessly placed people on the spot. "As you wish, Mr. Vilsak. Mrs. Bolton, please call the roll and record the vote."

Despite Nickerson's irritation with Melvin's request, the majority of those in attendance were pleased. The roll call added drama and excitement; the Dairy Queen could wait a few more minutes. Mrs. Bolton called the roll. With seven votes cast it was three ayes and four nays. Nickerson was sure that some had changed their positions in the roll call. Tom Leering was called on just before Nickerson. If Leering voted nay, it would be over, but to Nickerson's surprise, Tom Leering voted aye. Nickerson had the tie breaker. He paused, looked around the room, stared at Melvin, and bellowed, "Aye."

The audience of interested citizens seemed generally pleased with the vote. Although there were a few cat calls, there was a sense of relief and pending excitement. St. Luke, a small school district in central Minnesota, was about to step onto the national stage. With that reality now official, most people headed home, including Bobbie. Not wanting to drag the disappointment home with her, she called Barnes from her car. His response to her news was a simple, "Damn." With a heavy sigh and a change in his tone he asked, "How are you doing, Bobbie? I know this has been hard on you."

It took her a moment to gather her wits to respond to the soft side of Bruce Barnes. "I'm all right. Very disappointed but I appreciate your letting me handle this."

"Up to this point," Barnes said curtly, putting his personal side back under wraps.

"Bruce, this is a great district. Don't mess it up."

"Bobbie, we've had this discussion. We'll do what must be done with as little collateral damage as possible." The call was over.

Bobbie leaned her head against the steering wheel. A tear rolled out of each eye, one for the present, one for the past.

\* \* \*

WHEN THE MEETING ENDED, Melvin Vilsak had dashed out of the room. Jack shook as many of the board members' hands as he could. He spoke with Ken Keegan, thanked him for his support, and told him that the Aclare build-out team would be in touch tomorrow to begin the process of setting up the Aclare lab.

The boardroom was almost empty when Katy walked up to Jack. "I thought I should stay as a representative of the Gram family and congratulate you," she said as she shook his hand, "and thank you for making St. Luke such a priority."

"I'm very pleased and grateful for your father's support. Does Victor know?"

"He'll know first thing in the morning. I left him a voice mail. He's in bed already. He's got an early trip tomorrow."

"Yes, I know. I had dinner with him and Monsignor Murphy tonight."

"You did? How was it?"

118

"Wonderful. The conversation was excellent, and the fare superb. A local game bird your father had hunted."

"Pheasant, a treat of the northern prairie."

"Indeed," Jack said with his eyes locked on Katy's. "Does David know?"

"Oh, yes, I just phoned him. He's home with Anna."

"Well, please give him my thanks for encouraging me to attend tonight's meeting. I hadn't appreciated how important a personal touch is in St. Luke."

"This is small-town America," Katy said as she picked up her coat. "I imagine that personal touch will play well in St. Lukes from coast to coast."

"Yes, but I couldn't imagine sitting through board meetings in all seven thousand school districts with fewer than a thousand kids," Jack said as they walked to the parking lot.

"You won't have to, Jack. Your personal engagement here will transfer to other small districts. You've made an important statement by coming here twice."

"Three times," Jack corrected. "Don't forget the speeding ticket."

"Yes, three times," Katy said, smiling. "Where are you parked?"

"Too far away to be facing this wind," Jack said a little breathlessly.

"Minnesota. Wind is a way of life here. If you're planning to come back, at least before April, I strongly suggest a heavier coat."

Jack laughed as he wrapped his liner-less trench coat more tightly around him. "I'll keep that in mind."

"Now where did you say you parked?" Katy asked again.

"Let's see, the lot was full, so I parked there under the street light . . . oh, boy."

Katy and Jack stopped and stared. Jack pulled his hands from his coat and started to use his cell phone. Before them was Jack's rented car, four tires slashed, all windows broken.

A half hour later, the St. Luke police had completed their report. Katy had called David to let him know what had happened and that she would be late. With the police gone, Katy drove Jack to the Nightfall.

The two drove to the motel in silence. As Katy stopped her car to let Jack out, she asked, "How will you get to the airport tomorrow?"

"Don't worry about it. I'll have my assistant make arrangements."

"I could give you a ride," Katy offered.

Jack hesitated, then answered, "No, Katy, I couldn't ask that of you."

Katy insisted. "It wouldn't be any trouble. I'll just bundle up Anna and . . ." Katy didn't finish.

Jack placed his hand over Katy's as she held the parking brake. Their eyes locked. Jack opened the car door and walked into the Nightfall.

Chapter 16

# *Saturday of the Eighth Week of Football Season*

ACLARE'S FACILITIES TEAM called Ken Keegan the day after the vote. Within a week the future Aclare lab site had been measured for a retrofit. The two least desirable classrooms in the building had been offered for the pilot. The rooms were hot in fall and spring and freezing in winter. Because the windows had been covered in the energy-saving frenzy of the 1970s, the rooms were dark and water spots stained the tiled ceiling. David had taken English his freshman year in one of the rooms, but since he had been teaching at St. Luke, the rooms had been used for storage.

Renderings of the proposed Aclare lab were hung in the teachers' workroom, along with a position description for the lab director. As agreed in the contract, St. Luke could either provide a teacher to be trained in the Aclare method within ten days of the board's approval of the project, or Aclare would supply its own teacher.

David read the position posting. The skills addressed in the training seemed substantially different from those in his undergraduate classes or his administration training: logic and reasoning, analogies, intercultural communication, scripted instruction, systems thinking, spatial analysis, and mass customization. The training would take three weeks. By agreement with the St. Luke School Board, a substitute teacher would cover the classes for any teacher in the district that volunteered for the Aclare training, and a permanent sub would cover the spring semester.

David had never thought of leading the Aclare project, but the position description and renderings of the lab appealed to him. The idea of instructing and leading seventy-five students for the entire six-and-a-half-hour day didn't seem daunting but, rather, exhilarating. It seemed like a hi-tech, one-room schoolhouse where the students taught themselves and one another. Nevertheless, he pushed the thought of volunteering out of his mind when he realized that the training would conflict with the end of football season and the state playoffs.

No one stepped forward for the Aclare training. Discussion in the teachers' lounge focused on the 1:75 teacher to pupil ratio. "Bedlam," "chaos," "out of control" were some of the descriptions David heard from his colleagues. It was quite a surprise when Jack Taylor phoned him right after dinner that Saturday.

"Has anyone volunteered for the Aclare job, David?"

"Not yet, Jack."

"Why don't you do it? I think you'd be terrific."

"I must confess my interest, but football season isn't over, and then there are the playoffs."

"I see."

"I am about to step up to the . . ." David stopped.

"What's that, David?"

"Oh, nothing."

"Hey, here's an idea. If you do the Aclare training, bring Katy and Anna with you, and all of you can stay in our guest house. It's not very big, but at least you won't have to be away from them."

"But what about your family? Won't we be in the way?"

"Not at all. You can barely see the guest house from our home. It's a two-bedroom bungalow. It's never been occupied by an Aclare teacher trainee before, but I think your situation is unique."

"Jack, that's a very nice offer, but I haven't volunteered yet for the Aclare position."

"Hey, I like that word 'yet.' So it's just a matter of time?"

"I don't know."

"Look, talk it over with Katy. If you can't do it, I'll understand. We've got some great talent on our bench who can go to St. Luke if

122

need be, but I think your leadership would be very important to the pilot's success."

"Look, I'll give it some thought."

"I couldn't ask for more."

David hung up and began to clear the plates from the table. Katy came back in the kitchen. Anna had finished her supper by rubbing butter in her hair, so Katy had taken Anna for a bath and an early bedtime. "Who called?" she asked.

"That was Jack Taylor." Katy looked at David with a quizzical expression. "He's encouraging me to lead the Aclare pilot."

"What did you tell him?"

"I told him I'd think about it."

"Did you tell him about the end of the season and playoffs?"

"Yeah, sure!"

"Did you tell him that the greatest coach in Minnesota high school football was about to resign and you'll ascend to the throne?"

"Well," David hesitated, "no."

"Why not?"

"I'm not sure why, honey."

"What do you mean?"

David put the dirty dishes on the counter and sat back down at the table with a heavy sigh. "Katy, I felt like a jocko socko telling Taylor I couldn't participate in something as exciting as Aclare because of football. Something's happening, Katy, and I can't quite get my finger on it. I love football, honey. It's always been a part of my life. I love the game and the strategy. I love coaching and working with the players. You help the kids in lots of ways. You teach them about life on and off the field. I know that sounds trite, but good coaches do that. You help the guys build their strength, their leadership, their teamwork. You help them make better decisions, respond to pressure, think many steps ahead."

Katy sat down across from David. "Everything you're saying is true and good. So what's wrong?"

"Katy, I don't want to be head coach."

"I'm not surprised to hear you say that, David. You said something the other night that made a lot of sense, and I told you I wasn't surprised then. But what's all the internal conflict about? Carl will get over it if you don't take the job."

"I'm not so sure about that, Katy."

"What do you mean?"

"Well, Carl's a very gifted football coach. I think he could have easily coached at the college level. But he found his niche at St. Luke and has never looked beyond this community, although he sure had his chances. Anyway, football, like other sports, is really an oral tradition. You learn from those who went before you. The elders share their insights and experience with the next generation. They pass on their knowledge and their playbooks in this tacit, unspoken, but understood manner. We don't think about it as a tradition or a ritual, but it certainly is. It's a clear and defined culture. By not wanting the head job, I'm breaking that culture, a culture I love and that's been very good to me."

"You know, I've never quite seen it that way, David. But now that you put it in words, it makes sense. But I still think Carl will understand."

"I don't think so, Katy. This is the only culture Carl knows. He and I have never really talked about this culture or me stepping up. It's just been assumed. It's just been assumed I'd absorb the wisdom and take the leadership when the old chief dies or gets killed or drifts off on an iceberg."

"That sounds mighty tribal."

"That's it, Katy!" David exclaimed. "That's a perfect word for it. Tribal. Sports teams are tribal and have loads of unwritten rules, codes, and expectations as well as a hierarchy of dominance. But I'm getting lost in the weeds here, honey. The culture of sports is nothing new to me or to mankind. I'm just very aware that I'm considering leaving it."

"But people leave sports every day to do other things. You have a life to live as you see fit. Once a football player does not mean always a football player."

"I agree, honey, but there's more that's pushing me away, and this area is less defined. I haven't thought it through, but it's really churning in me."

"Okay, what's churning in you?" Katy asked as she sat back in her chair.

David stood up and resumed cleaning off the kitchen table. Katy watched him work. After things were put back into the refrigerator, David began to rinse the dishes. He turned on the water and stared out the window at the yard and the neighbors' homes. Then he turned to face Katy, who was patiently waiting. Leaning back on the counter and drying his hands he said, "When I was in high school, I played football, but that was my only sport. I was plenty good enough to play basketball and baseball, but I didn't. I needed to work. So from the time I was fourteen until I went to Iowa, I worked at the grocery store, you know, to help with my mom's medical bills.

"Football taught me a lot, but working at the grocery store taught me a lot too. And maybe not playing other sports kept me from getting hurt and let me channel all my athletic skill into football. It's hard to say. But I can say that it's not that way anymore."

"And what do you mean by that?"

"Today kids go from sport to sport to sport. It never ends. Sports dominate students' lives. Sports dominate families' lives. It starts when they're tiny tikes, not much older than Anna. We have soccer leagues that suck kids out of the neighborhoods and put them in organized sport. We have tee-ball and gymnastics and swimming teams right here in little bitty St. Luke. It happens from coast to coast in America, and that's even before the middle and high schools really get cranking on interscholastic athletics."

"I know what you mean. It drives me nuts to see the soccer fields jammed with cars every Saturday," Katy said.

"You know, you don't see children playing on their own outside anymore. There aren't any sandlot baseball games or pick-up basketball games at the park. Heck, kids rarely play in the park or in their yards or in their driveways. We've scheduled creativity and playtime out of our children's lives. We overprogram our kids. I don't know if we do this because we're so afraid of pedophiles, or because both parents work and there's no one home in the afternoons, or—to expand on what Carl said—because 'Sports hold schools together.' Maybe sports even hold our society together. I don't know. It's probably all of the above. Regardless, I don't want to participate in that culture any longer. At least I don't want to lead that culture as a head football coach."

"David, you don't have to be part of that anymore. It's your choice."

David sat down. "There's another part of this sports culture that really bothers me. The weight training program we put the football players through is nuts. Sure, it helps the kids play stronger, but for most of them, we've just added five or ten or, in some cases, twenty or thirty pounds that help on the football field. But after football is over, which will be twelfth grade for most kids, it will turn to flab. Those kids will lug around a butt-load of extra weight on torn-up knees for the rest of their lives. What kind of insanity is that?" David blew out a long breath and returned to the sink.

"Honey, it's all right to criticize the culture that's been good to you."

"I hadn't anticipated this fall bringing such change. If Aclare hadn't shown up, I would probably have gone along, never looking outside of what I do every day, being self-satisfied and blissful in my ignorance. I wouldn't have thought that education, that learning, is so much more than what we provide in the school building; that sport is the tail that wags the dog; that how things are today doesn't have to dictate how they'll be tomorrow, that Anna won't have to go to school in the same manner, with the same structure and curriculum as her grandfather and great-grandfather. Katy, I've got to tell Carl, and he won't understand."

David felt Katy hug him from behind, her hands under his shirt and her body pressed against his.

"What does this mean about Aclare?"

"I want to do it, Katy. Schooling in this country has to change. It has to become better, more meaningful. We're really pretty lucky in

St. Luke, but nationally we've got a forty percent drop-out rate. That spells long-term disaster. It means America will become just another mediocre nation. It means millions of people, young people, being far less than they could be, victims of a school system focused more on the well-being of adults than the well-being of the students."

"Okay, I've got a fired-up husband, who I'm going to miss while he goes to Aclare training."

"Well, you may have to miss me for two weeks but not three."

"How's that? I thought you said a week in San Francisco and two weeks at an Aclare school. That sounds like three weeks of missing you for me," Katy said, nibbling on his right ear.

"Yeah, but not only did Jack encourage me to take the Aclare position, he sweetened the deal by offering his guest house for you, Anna, and me while I train in San Francisco."

"His guest house?"

"Jack says it's a cozy two-bedroom bungalow, whatever a bungalow is, that you can barely see from his house."

"What did you say to him?"

"I told him I'd think about it. And what do you think about it, Mrs. Anderson?"

"I need to think about it as well. Anna's too young to appreciate San Francisco, but the three of us could have our evenings together. I just don't know what Anna and I would do for a week outside of our routine here, our walks and grocery shopping, her naps."

"What? My clear-headed wife is uncertain! That's different. I believe it would be a great break from the everyday for you."

"You're right, David. Let's go," Katy said with a burst of enthusiasm. She hugged David and whispered in his ear. *"Oui, partons en voyage à l'Ouest."*

David picked Katy up and sat her on the countertop. He leaned into her. "I don't know what you said, but I like it," he said as he twisted the blinds closed over the kitchen sink.

127

# Chapter 17

# *Monday of the Ninth Week of Football Season and through the Football Playoffs*

IT WAS MONDAY OF THE NINTH WEEK of football season. Carl and David were on the dock fishing, getting ready to watch some film after a decent practice. Katy was not at the Tuckers' for the second Monday in a row. Bobbie had broken more than a salad bowl two weeks ago. It was a crisp night, but the lack of wind made fishing possible. David didn't rant about sports wagging the dog or about weight training. He simply said, while threading a worm on his hook, "Carl, I don't want to take over for you next year." The statement slipped out coolly and calmly while Carl stared at his bobber in the water.

"I was afraid that was coming."

"What? You knew I was going to say that?"

"David, I've known you since you were twelve years old. I can read you like a book. Something's been brewing in you lately."

"It's that obvious?"

"Look, nobody says you have to take the head coaching position. I can't blame you for not wanting it. With all modesty aside, I'm a tough act to follow. It's a great trivia question to name the first five coaches that followed Bear Bryant at Alabama. But you've got what it takes. You know football, you're an excellent teacher, the kids respect you. Hell, you could've been head coach years ago at any school in the area."

David sat speechless with half a worm wiggling on his hook. He hadn't expected Carl to be understanding. After several minutes of silence, he replied, "I thought you should know before you make your announcement after the game on Friday."

"I appreciate you letting me know. I was pretty sure you were going to tell me this, and I figured that possibility into my plans."

"What's that mean?"

"That means I won't announce my retirement on Friday night."

David's stomach tightened. He felt like he had just denied his friend and mentor his long sought retirement and the rarest of all goals, retirement after a perfect season.

"Carl, I'm sorry. I didn't mean to screw up your plans."

"Hey, you're not screwing up anything. This team just might be good enough to take state even without the incentive of winning it for me. Hell, I might just stick around a few more seasons. Shit, I'm only fifty-five. Now that I've made the Rule of 85, I can retire anytime I choose. Maybe I'll coach until Bobbie makes her Rule of 85. That will give me time to break in a new assistant. I take it you're joining the family business. Victor's offered you a six-figure vice-presidency of something and wants to groom you to take over the company. I can't blame you for taking it."

"No, Carl, Victor doesn't see me as his successor."

Carl reeled in his line to check his bait. He looked up at David for the first time. "Then what's up?"

David had thought he had slid home safely. As long as Carl thought David was joining Gram Industries, he was happy for his protégé. David mentally tightened his chin strap and said, "Carl, I'm volunteering to lead the Aclare pilot. I've got to go to California next week to start training. I'll miss the playoffs."

Carl sat motionless, and then his hands began to quiver, the rod shaking madly. Taking the handle of the rod in his left hand and the middle of the rod in his right, he bent it until it snapped. Carl sat motionless again and let the broken rod and reel slowly slip through his hands and splash into the water. "Ah, shit, son, why'd you want to do that? Did Victor put you up to it?" Carl growled.

"No, Victor doesn't know."

Carl stood up and kicked the five-gallon bucket they used to hold their catch ten yards out into the lake. As Carl's foot pushed in the side of the bucket, two crappies flopped onto the wooden slats of the dock and lay gasping for air. David picked them up and dropped them back into the water.

"Why in the fuck would you want to do that? Aclare's nothing but a scam on public education, and Jack Taylor is scum. He's an opportunist who'll grab whatever he can whenever he can. That bastard's caused me so much grief. He's distracted the community, he's made my wife's life hell, and now he's taken my assistant coach and fucked up my retirement plans. How can you do this to Bobbie and me?"

"Carl, I never dreamed you'd be this upset."

"Upset? I'm way beyond upset. I want you to leave. We don't need to watch film tonight, and you don't need to come to practice tomorrow or ever again."

"Carl, I—"

"Don't say anything. Just leave."

Carl turned his back to David and walked to the end of the dock. The Saturday after the last game of the season, David usually helped Carl lift the dock out of the water before the ice set in. David wondered if he'd be participating in that annual ritual, next week or ever again. He laid his rod down. The bobber was dipping under the surface. He walked off the dock and said, "Carl, I'm sorry. You've got a bite."

At home Katy listened and rubbed David's shoulders as he told her how Carl took the news. She could hear the pain in David's voice and feel the hurt in his shoulders. David loved Carl in a way that men who rarely express their emotions love one another. Carl had coached David to a Big Ten scholarship, and together they had made a formidable coaching team. For that love, that bond, to be shattered was more than David could bear. He put his head on his knee and sobbed. Katy placed her head on David's and wept with him.

\* \* \*

The Taylor bungalow was anything but plain. It was beautifully appointed, comfortable, and private. David, Katy, and Anna arrived Sunday afternoon after a Saturday of getting over the shock of not being on the Letterman sideline the evening before. Rather than sit in the stands and create a stir, David stayed home Friday night and listened on the radio. Even over the radio, he could feel the opposing coaches' outrage and embarrassment as Carl ran the score up on his hapless opponent. A 63 to 0 drubbing was not entertaining for the home crowd and angered the visiting parents. David had said to Katy that he knew those kids from Cold Spring were bearing the brunt of Carl's anger at him. Carl was demonstrating that he could run the show just fine all alone.

As planned, the Andersons joined Jack and Rebecca Taylor and their six children for supper on Sunday night in their home. It was a wonderful evening. Anna sat in the hand-me-down high chair that had served the Taylor family, and she was the focus of everyone's attention. Rebecca Taylor was delightful, down-to-earth, and an excellent cook.

Over dinner David learned more about the itinerary he had received several days earlier. Jack gave him insights into the training system and each instructor. Rebecca and Katy talked like old friends about motherhood, San Francisco, and the Catholic Church.

It was nearing nine o'clock, and David and Katy were saying their thanks and goodnights to the Taylors when Anna grabbed a wine glass with a tablespoon of merlot still in it, raised it to her mouth, and poured it down the front of her pretty dress. Rebecca responded calmly, "Katy, take Anna to the powder room. Jack, get the stain remover from above the washer."

Katy had just pulled the wine-stained dress over Anna's head when Jack walked into the powder room. "Here's the stain stick," Jack said.

"Thanks," Katy responded as she rubbed it on Anna's dress and then tucked it into the diaper bag, "and thanks for a lovely evening."

"It was our pleasure. I'm so glad you came with David. I hope you have a week of perfect peace. Rebecca will certainly enjoy your company and having a baby in the house."

"You have a beautiful family, Jack."

"Thank you, and I say this with sincerity and affection, a spark doesn't have to start a fire."

"I couldn't agree more," Katy smiled with a sign of relief. Then whispered, "I like things that are closed in a single sentence."

"Enjoy your time here. David will get put through the paces during the day and he'll have a little reading every night, but he'll be home by four every—"

"Did you get the stain remover on?" Rebecca asked from the door of the powder room.

"It's going to be just fine. I'm sure the wine will come out, but if it doesn't, we'll have a nice reminder of a great evening."

As they walked to the back door, Rebecca stopped abruptly. "Oh, I almost forgot." She reached for an envelope on the expansive desk she had built into the kitchen cabinetry. "Here, take this. It's our schedule for the next week. With a family this large and our children so involved with school and activities, I need a schedule to keep everything straight. And it helps Jack know what's going on here when he's on the road. As you can see, he's gone Tuesday through Thursday of this week."

Katy looked at the schedule. It was incredible, showing piano lessons, basketball practice, furnace repairman, eye doctor appointments, haircuts, grocery shopping, morning Mass, gardening, and every known event of the coming week including supper menus. "Please don't think I'm nuts or some type of control freak for doing this; it just helps us protect family time."

"Looks like a great idea to me," Katy said. "The Anderson family hasn't quite developed the need for such a tool in either volume or age, but give us time."

"Thanks. That's nice of you to say, especially when you're probably thinking 'this woman is nuts.' But notice the supper menus. You're welcome to join us any evening. Wednesday will be Mexican night. The kids love it, and Jack hates it. Come any night; there's always plenty. But save Friday night for the four of us to go to our favorite dinner and dance place. Now run along, or we'll have you up all night."

As they walked to the guest house Katy said, "Rebecca Taylor is one organized woman."

To which David replied, "Organized and beautiful. Pretty much like the woman I married."

"David, I don't hold a candle to her skills."

"Oh, yes, you do. You just haven't had to manage a house with six kids. Yet."

Katy pulled closer to David and he wrapped his arm around her, holding Anna on his other shoulder.

* * *

THE WEEK IN SAN FRANCISCO was fast and enriching. Jack introduced David around the Aclare office on Monday morning and then turned him over to the trainers, the most performance-focused educators David had ever met. Every session whether on technology, content, or sequencing focused on what it meant for the students and the expected outcome. David spent about a third of the week learning about the technology, trouble shooting, and weekly maintenance. The other two-thirds of the week provided the best, most in-depth immersion in learning theory and scope-and-sequence that he had ever had.

Jack Taylor had selected his Aclare trainers for their breadth and depth of knowledge and for their ability to teach teachers. Each trainer had spent at least a year teaching at an Aclare school, and each held a doctorate in curriculum and instruction.

At the end of the week, David had greatly expanded the smattering of learning theory he had been exposed to at Iowa and St. Cloud State and had received substantial grounding in multiple intelligences, critical thinking, asymmetrical learning, information absorption, and another dozen ideas that served as the backbone of the Aclare process.

Katy had found herself enjoying the break from her St. Luke routine. She and Anna took long walks through the Taylors' secluded neighborhood. They had the heated pool and the entire pool house all to themselves. Katy even gardened on Tuesday and Thursday morning with Rebecca. The Taylors had five acres manicured to perfection, all at Rebecca's direction. Their gardener and his three helpers spent each Tuesday and Thursday working on the yard. Rebecca, who was a master gardener and was on the board of the San Francisco Botanical Garden, spent three hours both mornings with her crew, working harder and getting dirtier than her hired help.

For Katy it was inspirational to see how Rebecca had transformed what had formerly been five acres of mowed grass and a few trees into a place of privacy, beauty, and peace. A full acre was devoted to a field for the kids' games, and it too was manicured and screened with hedges from neighboring properties.

While walking the yard, moving rocks, and planning with the gardener, Katy and Rebecca carried on a rich conversation. Rebecca Taylor was every bit as talented as her better-known spouse. Most impressive was how much she accomplished in a day or a week and how little of it was devoted to herself but rather done for the good of others. The other feature that struck Katy was how Rebecca had raised her children to be just like her—simple, giving, and responsible. Rebecca may have had a gardener, but she surely didn't have a maid, a cook, a housekeeper, or a nanny. Doing mundane chores—cleaning bathrooms, sweeping floors, preparing meals—were sanctifying events for Rebecca, prayers, a building of her faith and family.

On Friday night, the Taylor girls, little Marie and her big sister, Marta, came to the guest house to babysit Anna. Jack, just back from his business trip, and Rebecca took Katy and David out for dinner and dancing. Over dinner David learned where he would do his classroom training.

"David, I'm excited to tell you that your next two weeks of training will take place in Washington, D.C.," Jack said.

"That'll be great," David responded. "How did D.C. get picked?"

"Well, we can train a future Aclare teacher at any of our schools that have been operating for a full year. But I want you to see our D.C.

schools. No matter where you go, you're going to see schools that look radically different from St. Luke. I have absolute confidence that Aclare will thrive in St. Luke under your leadership.

"The trainers said you set a new standard for Aclare teachers. I want you to go to D.C. for two reasons. First, it's one of the most fouled-up and expensive school districts in America. As a comparison to St. Luke, it's the other end of the scale on nearly any measure. You'll learn a lot just by being there. You'll also learn a lot about St. Luke. Second, I've got to be in D.C. sometime over the next two weeks, and we can have dinner."

"Great."

"Aclare will put you up at the University Club under my membership. It's just a few blocks from the White House and about a twenty-minute walk to Radford High School, an Aclare partner. Katy, I hope you and Anna won't miss David too much."

"Oh, we'll miss him terribly, but we'll be fine."

"Good, I know you're flying back to Minnesota tomorrow." Jack reached into his inside pocket and handed David an envelope. "Take Monday to enjoy being home. Fly to D.C. on Tuesday and report to Radford on Wednesday morning. All the details are in this envelope, including your airline ticket and confirmation for the University Club. I've made reservations for us to have dinner Thursday night in the Taft dining room at the University Club. Usually the people in training get to go home for the weekend, but I hope you'll be willing to stay. There's a fundraiser for Congressional Republicans on Friday night I'd like you to attend."

"Sounds fine."

"And I'm hoping you won't mind joining me in hosting several members of the California Congressional delegation who'll be my guests at the 49ers–Redskins game."

"Hey, tough duty, but I'll be glad to do it." David grinned.

"I figure you can add some real insight to the game."

"Well, it's a bit of a jump from the St. Luke Lettermen to the NFL, but I'll do what I can."

"Hey, enough work. Let's enjoy ourselves. This is our favorite spot. We've been coming here for years and always have a great time. We're so glad you could join us." Jack proposed a toast. "To health, wealth, and God's blessings on the Andersons."

The dinner was marvelous, and conversation was not about Aclare. As dessert was served, a quintet struck up their first tune. "Oh," Rebecca said, "a rumba. Let's go." She grabbed Jack's hand and said, "Come on, Mr. and Mrs. Anderson." David and Katy looked at each other and gulped. They had hardly danced together in their entire relationship; a few flings at Iowa and at their wedding, but they weren't really dancers.

Jack and Rebecca were already on the floor. It was clear they loved dancing. They were smooth and elegant. Katy and David stole to a quiet corner of the dance floor. David's legs felt tight. He wanted to loosen up, stretch out, but that didn't seem appropriate. His mouth turned dry. He felt like he'd just run the steps at Kinnick Stadium. Katy was more at ease and whispered, "Hey, I think we've been caught with our dance down. We've got nothing to lose."

When they finally found their rhythm, David and Katy did fine with the basics, but this crowd, and especially Jack and Rebecca, were well ahead of the basics. After the first number ended, David and Katy sat down while Jack and Rebecca continued to dance. After the next dance, the Taylors returned to the table. Rebecca took David's hand, and Jack took Katy's. For the next half hour the four danced non-stop.

"Gosh, we should probably get back to Anna," Katy said.

"Let's just dance a few more," Jack said. "We'll leave in fifteen minutes. Anna's in great hands with Marta. I'm sure Marie is fast asleep on the guesthouse sofa."

"Sounds great," responded David, "but please excuse me for a moment." Jack led Katy to the dance floor while David headed for the restroom. As he returned, he stopped near the bar and watched Jack and Katy dance a tango.

* * *

WASHINGTON OPENED DAVID'S EYES. He was shocked by the condition of Radford High and the rampant disrespect and other negative attitudes of the students. He walked to Radford each day, the last four blocks feeling unsafe, but never had a problem on the street.

The four Aclare labs at Radford were oases of calm and learning inside a desert of wasted time and lives. David was already a believer in Aclare, but Radford tipped him from believer to crusader.

Growing up in St. Luke, he'd never seen urban poverty or hopelessness such as he found not two miles from the White House. Every day he thought of the old black woman he had met at the Aclare reception, Viola Fulghum, who attended just to tell anyone she could how Aclare had saved her grandson's life, the woman Bobbie thought was an actor. Now David understood.

On Thursday David and Jack had dinner in the Howard Taft dining room. After catching up, the conversation turned to the politics of Aclare. "David, I'm glad you stepped up to lead our program in St. Luke."

"Well, as I've said before, I'm interested and happy to do it. Believe me, I haven't changed my mind."

"No, and I don't want to wear you out with my thanks, but the reason I wanted to have dinner with you tonight is to talk one on one. I know you just spent a week at my guesthouse, but the time you and I had together always involved our wives and/or children. Wonderful time, but not the best for business discussions."

"Understood."

"David, right now you're an Aclare trainee, but I think your future with Aclare is bright and unlimited."

David sat back and laughed. "I surely didn't expect that. But tell me more."

"There's no doubt that our approach gets far better results than traditional educational practices and structures. Even our enemies accept that. It's critical that our teachers continue to do outstanding jobs for our students. Your training and your leadership in St. Luke will give you the experience you need to understand Aclare's structure and its effect on students in a real, not theoretical, setting."

"Sure, I'm with you so far, but you have lots of great teachers already in your operation. I'm working with several top-notch people at Radford."

"You're right, David. We do have some great people at Radford, but you'll find great people in any Aclare program. What we've been able to do is run a highly effective program with average to good teachers. If we had to start with superstar teachers, the model wouldn't work. Our model can get great results with average teachers. That's part of its beauty. Average teachers can be found anywhere. Superstars are much harder to find."

"Okay, but the Radford teachers look like stars to me."

"That's great to hear. It means our program's working. The teachers at Radford, when they volunteered to lead the Aclare lab, were ordinary classroom performers. But with our brief training and our structure, they moved from being mediocre teachers to teaching champions."

"How do you explain that transformation?"

"Two things. Most of the teachers who volunteer to run an Aclare lab are unhappy with their current teaching situation. I think Aclare gives them a happier teaching environment—less prep time, fewer discipline problems, really engaged students. Well, you know the drill."

"Right, but what's the second reason?"

"They get revived, energized by the environment, the students, the success they have. While they may not be superstars, they still become highly effective, and that's how we get great results with average teachers."

"Okay, but given what we've just discussed, why is my future with Aclare so bright?"

"Because you, David, came to Aclare as a superstar."

"What?"

"Our people in San Francisco said you were the best teacher they'd trained in the program. You're experienced, exceptionally well read, a clear decision maker, very curious, and an excellent communicator—all traits of a good leader. Your own football career and your years of coaching are terrific background for Aclare. You've even been nominated for this year's Minnesota Teacher of the Year Award."

"How do you know that?"

"Your lovely wife bragged about you."

"Well, now that I've volunteered for Aclare, I think I can kiss good-bye any chance I might have had for that award."

"That's too bad, David. I hope Aclare will more than compensate the disappointment. Changing the subject just a bit, I was impressed with you when I first met you at the rally. I was amazed you weren't working for Victor."

"You know, I've never really thought about working for him. Funny, you're the second person who recently presumed I should work for Victor."

"Oh, yeah? Who's the other insightful person?"

"Carl Tucker, St. Luke's head football coach."

"That's interesting. Why does he think you belong at Gram Industries?"

"Well, a couple of weeks ago I told him I wasn't planning to take the head coaching job when he retires. My statement didn't faze him. He assumed I was going to work for Victor. But when I told him I was going to lead the Aclare lab, all hell broke loose."

"Why?"

"It's a long story, but Carl thinks you've screwed up his life. You distracted the community during football season, and you caused problems for his wife—she heads the local teachers association. I guess the final straw was you stealing his protégé."

"Sorry about that. I didn't mean to cause him trouble. If you've coached with him, he must be a fine man."

"The finest and a great friend. It's been tough the last few weeks."

139

During dinner David told Jack about life in St. Luke over the last two months. He talked about the Tuckers and how strained things had become. He noted Carl's soliloquy on sports—football first, basketball second—being the glue holding public education together, to which Jack laughed and said he'd never thought about it but agreed. David told Jack about all the discussion in town and in the teachers' room about Aclare and described the trip to the gala and the Sharon Lunsford affair tale.

"David, this gives me a glimpse into the controversy Aclare creates in a community. Hearing it personalized and on such a small scale as St. Luke means a great deal."

"Jack, there are a couple of things I saw at the gala I'd like to ask you about."

"Shoot."

"First, before your speech, I met two men at the cocktail hour who represented the teachers' organizations. I was surprised when they told me that each of their organizations own a substantial number of shares of Aclare."

"You must mean Tim Jenson and Sam Block."

"Exactly. I'd forgotten their names."

"They come to every public event, try to get face time with me, drink a lot of wine, and then report back to their organizations."

"With the exception of drinking a lot of wine, that's exactly what they told me they did," David laughed.

"So what about them?"

"Well, when you mentioned in your address that you had brought in investors from China, those two guys ran out of the ballroom like their pants were on fire."

Jack smiled and tilted his head with a satisfied look. "I didn't know that! The lights in my eyes made it hard to see the audience. Oh, I wish I had seen them run out! That would have really felt good."

"Why? I don't understand."

"Well, the two teachers associations and many of their state affiliates own Aclare stock."

"Interesting, but I still don't see why they own something that's antithetical to their interests."

"I like the word 'antithetical.' They may not like what we do, but if they continually ratchet up their ownership of Aclare, they could create havoc for us. The unions have huge amounts of money to invest. They use a tiny slice of that for riskier investments like Aclare. Anyway, these state organizations will buy a position, always small enough that they don't have to register their action with the SEC."

"I understand that, but how does selling the Chinese a chunk of the company change things?"

"It helps in several ways. First, the Chinese purchase soaks up a good bit of the stock available for purchase. That makes the stock more valuable because there's less of it. Second, the Chinese investors get a board seat. To date, Aclare's been pretty closely held, and I've had a very friendly board. Bringing in the Chinese definitely makes me more accountable to my shareholders. Third, and the key reason, the teachers associations love picking on me, but now every action they take will also affect the Chinese investors, and the unions don't want to piss off a group like Zhou Wu Limited. They are huge, with investments across the American markets. If they see that type of B-school shenanigans by the teachers' associations, they, the teachers, will have hell to pay. There's going to be a lot of overlap between Zhou Wu's holdings and the teachers' funds. Again, the teachers don't want to piss off Zhou Wu."

"So you courted the Chinese investors to fence out the teachers?"

"Actually, that was a fortunate side benefit. I courted the Chinese because their school market is almost ten times the size of that of the U.S." There was a slight pause, then Jack said, "Did you have a second question?"

"Oh, yeah," David shook his head. "At the reception before your speech, Bobbie, my colleague who heads the St. Luke teachers association, and I met a frail black grandmother who said her grandson had been saved by Aclare. She also said she saves her Social Security to make every Aclare meeting."

"You met Viola Fulghum."

"That's right. Well, Bobbie thought Viola was an actress you pay to play that role. Is Viola for real?"

"She's for real, all right. But you said she told you she saves her Social Security to pay for the trip?"

"That's what she told us."

"That's not true. I pay her to be there. She's certainly no actress, but she can C.O.D, that's cry on demand. When I met her at a meeting in Maryland and later verified the story of her grandson, I made an arrangement with her to attend our rallies and tell her tale. I'll have to ask her to stop the Social Security part. She gets first-class airfare and top-flight accommodations plus a thousand dollars. I think her story's worth every penny."

David was disappointed but worked hard not to show it. Not only had Jack paid Viola to attend, but also Bobbie had sniffed her out as a plant, whereas he had been duped.

"Interesting," David said as he noticed a couple being seated at a corner table. The woman's back was to David, but she still seemed familiar. No, it couldn't be, David thought as he worked to turn his attention back to Jack.

"What's up? Someone you know?" Jack asked, indicating the people at the corner table.

"I'm not sure."

"Well, they look like two people who have a lot of interest in one another. Why don't you go over and say hello before they get so engrossed that you spoil the romance."

David walked toward the couple thinking it couldn't be, but as he saw her in profile, he was sure it was her. He approached the table. "Sharon?"

She turned her head. "David?" Then she jumped out of her seat and hugged him, kissing him on the lips. "What are you doing here?"

"I was going to ask you the same thing. But being Minnesota nice, I'll tell you first."

"Oh, I miss Minnesota nice. David you're so sweet."

Jack Taylor was taking this all in with a chagrined look.

"Well, I'm in D.C. doing some training for Aclare."

"I think it's great that St. Luke approved the pilot," Sharon said.

"Yes, and I'll lead the lab, thus the training. What are you doing in Washington?"

"I'm just focused on the new job I took that forced me to resign my teaching position. I do miss my students, but I also really love what I'm doing now. Oh, David, it's so good to see you! Please say hello to everyone in St. Luke." She kissed him again, this time on his cheek, and returned to her dinner companion.

David went back to the table with Jack. "So, who's the lovely lady?" Jack asked.

"That's Sharon Lunsford."

"The woman who tried to bag you in San Francisco?"

"Yep."

"You've got more will power than me."

"What's she doing here?"

"Working, so she says, for whom I don't know."

"Do you recognize her dinner companion?"

David looked at the man and said, "No."

"I don't either."

David mused, "I guess I interrupted a business dinner."

"I'm sure you did, my friend. I'm sure you did."

David saw Sharon twice more that weekend, once at the Congressional fundraiser for the Democrats, where she was on the arm of a Congressman from Wisconsin, and again at the Redskins game. Both times she greeted David with a hug and a kiss.

# Chapter 18

# *The Football Off-Season*

$\mathrm{D}$AVID HAD NEVER FELT TIME PASS more rapidly than it did with the Aclare project. Although he had seventy-five students the entire school day, he knew he was doing some of his most effective teaching. The students were engaged and enthusiastic.

The former storage rooms had been transformed into the nicest facilities in the high school. With indirect, diffused fluorescent lights and natural lighting from the eye-level windows that had been opened in the west wall, the lab was well lit. An air-moving system kept the room fresh and comfortable. Each student had a low-walled study carrel, desktop terminal, and adequate space, and the absence of piles of textbooks kept the lab clutter-free. It was similar to the labs in San Francisco and D.C. But this lab was his.

When David volunteered to lead the project at St. Luke, he received all types of comments from "Did Victor make you do it?" to "You must be out of your mind." Now that the lab was reality, he had a steady stream of colleagues dropping in after school to learn more about it. Though David felt like a crusader for Aclare, he tempered his enthusiasm for the benefit of his fellow teachers. He was not there to sell them on Aclare. Jack and Viola could do that. Besides, he was sure that the end of the year test scores would impress his colleagues.

As it turned out, during January and February David figured he had hosted almost every teacher and administrator in the district plus dozens of people from surrounding districts. Even the governor had toured with the state superintendent. Two names, however, were missing from those who had toured the Aclare lab: Carl and Bobbie Tucker.

There had been no interaction between the Tuckers and the Andersons since Carl's outburst at David's choice to lead Aclare. After that, David went for his training, then the holidays came, and the new semester started. For all the excitement David had for Aclare, heaviness and regret weighed on his heart for how things had changed with Carl and Bobbie. It appeared that their years of friendship were over simply because of his decision to work with Aclare. He knew the guilt he felt was out of place and wondered how he could have approached the situation differently so as to maintain their friendship.

Katy advised him to let it go; there was nothing he could have done that would have resulted in a different outcome. For reasons Katy still didn't understand, Bobbie's loyalty to the association trumped her love of the Andersons. It was a daily sadness that time would temper.

Carl didn't retire from the head coaching role. The Lettermen didn't win state. They lost in the playoffs while David was training in Washington, D.C. On the Friday after Thanksgiving, David cleared out his coaching office. In a town as small as St. Luke, it surprised David and Katy that they hadn't bumped into one or both of the Tuckers. Katy surmised the Tuckers were doing more than just keeping to themselves. They were avoiding the Andersons.

\* \* \*

JANUARY, FEBRUARY, AND MARCH went rapidly, David engrossed in Aclare and Katy preparing for her trip to France. The last week of April, Katy and the high school French teacher, Sara Jenkins, would fly with twelve students to Paris where they would spend two nights before going to Normandy and Brittany. Then they would turn south to Provence and learn about viticulture and the artists of southern France before heading home from Marseille. It was on this last leg of the trip that they would spend three nights at Jack Taylor's home.

David and Anna drove Katy to the high school on the date of her departure for France and hugged her before she boarded the yellow school bus for the drive to the Minneapolis airport. Katy was excited yet felt torn as a mother and wife. Sara had never been to France or traveled abroad, so from the beginning of the planning process, David was pleased to see Katy engaged in the trip. Katy's extensive traveling experience and excellent French would be huge benefits for everyone. Without Katy, David felt that the trip would not have taken place.

Sara was a good teacher for those few students who stuck with French into their junior and senior years. She was a fortyish woman whose husband had died in a farming accident five years earlier. Katy, with a heart full of love, had become one of Sara's best friends and was the only person in St. Luke with whom Sara could converse in French. As much as Katy hated to leave David and Anna for the week, she wanted to support Sara. If Sara could get a first trip to France under her belt, then she'd be able to manage future trips on her own. Sara was timid but tough. Katy felt that coleading this trip was a gift to her friend, an opportunity for Sara to grow wings rather than more roots in the dirt of Minnesota.

Twelve students joined Katy and Sara, nine girls and three boys. In all of her travels to Paris, Katy had never seen the city in full spring bloom. It was breathtaking. She and Sara pressed the students to use their clumsy French even though English was widely used. The two days in Normandy and Brittany were vastly different from Paris, yet the students enjoyed these smaller towns. They were awed at the beaches of Normandy, and learning about the challenges that faced their grandfathers and, for some of them, their great-grandfathers' generation. Katy couldn't imagine the one senior and two junior boys on her tour tossing around in a landing craft off Omaha Beach about to be dropped into a sausage grinder of German fire. The Celtic roots of Brittany surprised the students despite their exposure to French history and culture back in St. Luke. Nonetheless, sitting in a pub until midnight listening to Celtic music in France was something none would forget.

The quality of the light in Provence stunned the students from Minnesota as they watched it sprinkle the vineyards and farmhouses. Though too young to drink more than a sample of the wines, the students scheduled a wine tour with Mrs. Jenkins while Katy had a day to herself. Katy and Sara had arranged this so that Sara could lead the group entirely on her own for a day.

With everyone else gone on the tour, Katy relaxed at the Provence home of Jack Taylor. It was not a small cottage as he had described it when they first met in Victor's study. But neither was it a huge home. It slept the fourteen members of the St. Luke party adequately, with the boys taking the sofas and carpets downstairs and the girls tripling up in the four bedrooms upstairs.

While in California for David's training, Katy had learned that Jack had inherited the house some twenty years ago. It served as the home base for the Taylor family on their European trips, three so far. Jack leased the use of the vineyards to area wine makers, but most of the time the house stood empty.

After a leisurely morning bath, Katy rode a bike into Toulon to enjoy a cup of coffee and to walk the streets without a crowd in tow. Toulon was warm, alive with light on this late morning in April. Katy enjoyed her coffee on the sidewalk, thinking of David and Anna still asleep in St. Luke. An hour later, she was buying bread as an evening snack for the students when someone in English said, "Now that's enough bread to feed a mighty big family." She turned. Her heart twinged to see Jack Taylor standing behind her.

"What are you doing here?"

"Well, the darnedest thing happened. I own a lovely home just a couple of miles . . . oh, let me say that more clearly . . . just three and a half kilometers from here. Back in the fall, I loaned the house for several nights to a high school group from Minnesota, never anticipating that I would be called by the local government here to deal with the property's tax status at the same time."

"Oh, my goodness. So you had to come to Provence to pay your property taxes?"

"It's something like that. But in truth," Jack paused, "If I hadn't known I might see you, I'd have simply had a local attorney handle it for me."

"I don't know whether to be flattered or worried. Friend and admirer flies halfway across the world to see me."

"I hope you're flattered."

Katy laughed and, with an armful of bread, gave him a hug, which he responded to with a kiss that lingered a bit long on the lips.

"Where are you staying? Is your family with you?"

"No, I'm alone. I was in New York when I decided to take care of the property problem. I called Rebecca to let her know what had come up. I'll head back to California in the next few days."

Katy felt a strange mixture of excitement and agitation. To meet up with Jack Taylor in Provence on her one free day was great in theory, but she thought Jack had closed that door in the powder room as she was cleaning Anna's dress. "A spark doesn't have to start a fire," he'd said. Katy had appreciated his candor. Now she wondered if that only applied on his home turf, his guesthouse, his time with his wife. Here in France were there no rules? No neighbors? No spouses? Was it open season on Katy?

"Join me for lunch?" Jack asked.

Lunch with Jack was difficult for Katy. For starters, it was totally unexpected. It was noontime, and Katy didn't like to drink before the late afternoon. That invariably gave her a headache. Even worse, Jack was very encouraging of David and his future with Aclare. Was that to gain access to her? To top it off, she felt that she looked great thanks to the color on her face from the Provence sun. Jack was clearly entranced. Despite her better judgment, she drank wine with her lunch, and Jack continually refilled her glass. Somewhere between what must have been her second and third glass of wine, Katy felt a tingle in her body that was reserved for David. She bent over and whispered in Jack's ear, "Where are you staying?"

"Le Rue Tab. Just two blocks away."

"I know the place. Give me fifteen minutes."

When Jack left, Katy got on her bike and rode not to Le Rue Tab but back to Jack's estate. She hoped he got her message. Whether their relationship was preserved didn't matter. She didn't want to tell him off. In fact she couldn't. Her attraction to him combined with her lunchtime wine made Katy rely on tricking him in order to gain the time and sobriety she needed to avoid a dreadful mistake. Katy was in love with David, actively and totally in love with David. She had had a child with him, and to violate the sanctity of her family for a cheap affair was vile, not of morning light. As she pedaled, she broke into a full sweat, letting the wine out of her body, letting Jack Taylor out of her mind. From the moment she had seen him in the bakery, she knew he had gone too far. It is one thing to feel. It is another thing to do.

Katy had been no chaste virgin when she married David, but at that moment of marriage, she formed a sacred bond with David that she would never break. Jack Taylor, inviting Katy and David into his home to meet his wife and children, was the lowest form of life in Katy's view. She was so angry and riding so intensely, she didn't see the baseball sized stone in the road which tipped her bike badly scraping her leg and twisting her ankle. As she soaked her injured leg in the tub at Jack's estate, she hoped he was sitting at the hotel at Le Rue Tab, realizing that she wasn't on her way, and receiving a none-too-subtle hint to leave her alone.

\* \* \*

ABOUT THE SAME TIME that the students were enjoying the bread Katy had bought for an evening treat, David was placing the bubble sheets from the Minnesota Academic Assessment Test into a manila envelope. The students had taken the test over the past three days, and David would turn in their score sheets the following morning. He was confident they would do well. He had seen tremendous growth in their ability to concentrate, problem solve, and think analytically. Even more astounding, the growth had been evenly spread across the students. Back in December more students had wanted to be in the Aclare program than there had been seats available, so a lottery was held. As a result, a true cross section of St. Luke students had populated the lab.

In just four months, David had watched his class grow from students who knew how to answer questions to students who knew how to think. It was a day-to-day process that showed remarkable results over the pilot period. As he was closing the metal clasp on the manila envelope that held the bubble sheets, the intercom from the office came on: "Mr. Anderson, please report to the office." The voice was male, almost familiar but out of place. He slid the tests in the drawer of his desk and headed for the office.

\* \* \*

THE PAST FEW MONTHS had been hell at the Tucker home. The loss of their friendship with David and Katy and their grandparent role with Anna hung heavily. Moreover, there was a tension between Carl and Bobbie that they had never experienced. Aclare had won its pilot program in the district, but something beyond that was menacing their peace.

Carl gave Bobbie a wide berth. The special education audit was conducted in March. In early April, the district received the audit report, and the multiple corrective actions began immediately. The process had been long and tedious, but Bobbie had done a fine job. No school district she was aware of had ever received a perfect score on this audit.

There were innumerable processes and procedures, and any auditor worth his or her salt knew how to find slips and technical violations. It was a game. Unless a district wantonly and ruthlessly ignored the rights of children with special needs, districts and auditors played cat and mouse. The districts did their best in applying and adhering to the federal regulations, and the auditors understood the complexities and challenges of applying the rules in the field.

Technically the auditors could create havoc for a district, but pragmatically they issued corrective actions and moved on. It was the same in district after district, state after state. Bobbie had spent hundreds of hours preparing for the report, but to what end? She knew the process and the auditor's report would not result in improved education for her students. Combining this with the pressure she felt from St. Paul about Aclare, she became increasingly weary. For the first time, she thought about the Rule of 85.

Bruce Barnes had been relentless in pressuring Bobbie, yet she had kept him out of the school board vote. Now she regretted that move. Had the pilot never been approved, her life would have been better. If she had let Barnes participate more in the strategy to keep Aclare out, even if it had been approved, she would have been in a better position. As it was, Barnes kept telling Bobbie to, "Assure its failure . . . Kill it in the crib . . . Under no circumstances must the Aclare contract be extended. You, Bobbie, must handle this."

Bobbie was in knots. She didn't know how to discredit the Aclare pilot; she didn't even want to think about how to spoil it. But she had no choice. Bruce Barnes had threatened the nuclear option. She was pinned.

Bobbie Tucker was a good woman, a loving wife, an effective teacher, a community leader; but in the mid-'70s she had made one terrible mistake. She had had a brief but torrid affair with Bruce Barnes. It was after his wife had been killed in a traffic accident, before he was president of the association, and during a period of dramatic teacher unrest in Minnesota. That summer she had spent weeks in St. Paul on a state strategy team, coordinating strikes across the state. Over fifty districts opened school late that fall, but the association had established itself as a force in Minnesota. In those heady, passionate, and sweltering days she lost her bearings and her fidelity to Carl. She became pregnant by Bruce, and in the fall of that year, she took a week off—for what she told Carl and the school district were Association meetings in St. Paul— to have an abortion that left her unable to have children. Bobbie was remorseful for her mistake. She never told Carl and she re-devoted herself to him, letting football and his love of the outdoors define their marriage. She kept their love life active and energetic when other couples around them seemed to lose interest in one another. She used the Barnes affair as a platform to improve Carl's life. But that platform had a flaw, a fissure, a fault.

In mid-March, the stress of Aclare mounted, and Bobbie hit a serious depression. She held herself together at work, but at home she cried constantly. Carl listened and encouraged her to perk up. He attributed her sadness to the gray weather that had uncharacteristically hung over Minnesota for much of February and March. He felt certain Bobbie would be her old self by April as spring came.

But on a weekend at the end of March, Bobbie hit bottom. Carl wondered if he should take her to the hospital. He knew then that this was more than just a response to overcast skies. As he held his crying, depressed wife, he realized that it was the Aclare pilot and the pressure from St. Paul taking its toll. He learned that St. Paul had demanded the pilot's failure. Carl, who thought in terms of plays, offense, defense, camouflage, and the kill, took it upon himself to solve Bobbie's problem and bring her back from depression. With her head in his lap, he brushed her hair with his hand and said, "Bobbie, I understand your problem, and I'll fix it. Don't you worry. You just get back to feeling good, and ole Carl will take care of things." From that moment on, Carl was thinking about how to wreck the Aclare pilot and the dreams of his former assistant.

\* \* \*

WITH DAVID ON THE WAY to the administration office, Carl took out the manila envelope from the desk, emptied its contents of bubble sheets into his gym bag, and replaced them with ones he had painstakingly created for each student in the pilot program. Bobbie knew nothing of his plan. Carl had created all the individualized answer sheets in the boathouse over several weeks. Once his plan was devised, he had even mailed Bruce Barnes a three-by-five index card inside a check-sized envelope inside a number ten envelope marked "CONFIDENTIAL." On the index card was printed "Aclare will die" and signed "A friend." With the false sheets in the envelope, he returned it to David's desk and walked out of the room.

When David arrived at the office he told the school secretary, Sue Rogers, "I'm here."

Sue responded, "I can see that. Now tell me what for."

"I was just paged to come to the office."

"David, I'm the only one in the office and, except for a quick trip to the bathroom to, quote, 'powder my nose,' my little fingers and my not so little bootie have been in this chair getting ready to send our assessment tests in tomorrow because, if we get them in tomorrow, we get them back next week. Without bursting your bubble, I have to tell you no one called you to the office besides, you know, if you'd just leave Katy, you could have all of me." She let out a huge breath.

"Someone did, or else I'm just losing it," David smiled. "Oh, and thanks for that reminder about dumping Katy. Tempting, very tempting," he teased as he backed out of the office door. He turned to head to his classroom and bumped directly into Carl. "Carl, excuse me," David smiled uncomfortably.

"No, excuse me, David. I should have been looking where I was going," Carl blurted, with the real bubble sheets concealed in his bag just inches from David. Thinking quickly, Carl said, "Look, look, I was just on my way to your room. With all that's happened, I haven't seen you all winter, and I was wondering if you'd like to go out on the Opener."

Baffled, David replied, "Sure, Carl, that'd be great. The Opener's not this weekend but next, right?"

"You're right, David. Great then, I'll see you at 6:00 a.m. at the boathouse," Carl said as he continued walking in the direction he had been when David bumped into him.

"See you then," David said, puzzled that Carl was walking away from the Aclare classroom, not toward it, when they bumped into each other.

\* \* \*

KATY ARRIVED HOME THE NEXT EVENING. It was a joyous homecoming. David had supper prepared, and Anna sat in her mother's lap instead of her high chair. David heard all about the trip, the sights, the students, and Sara Jenkins' growth. "She's ready to do it again next year and lead the trip by herself. It was a great experience for her." Katy didn't tell David about Jack. There would be a better time for that. Besides, she didn't want to spoil her first night back.

After Anna was in bed, Katy asked, "So what's new in St. Luke?"

"Same old same old," David reported and then suddenly remembered, "But—news flash!—yesterday I literally bumped into Carl, and he asked if I'd join him for the Opener."

"That's good news. I take it you told him yes?"

"Six in the morning next Saturday."

\* \* \*

THE THURSDAY BEFORE THE FISHING OPENER, the assessment test scores arrived. By agreement between the school board and Aclare, in order to continue the Aclare program, students must have improved twenty percent from their previous year's performance. David was confident of the students' progress, yet he didn't see himself as the reason that they had grown so greatly. Rather, the Aclare program and the students deserved the credit. He had coached and encouraged his students, but they were really responsible for their own progress. David picked up his results in the office and hurried to the Aclare lab to review them. No students had yet arrived, and he looked forward to this private moment of triumph.

He could not have been more disappointed. The test results, which he had expected to show consistent growth across disciplines and skills, were wildly inconsistent. David was confused. He could see no pattern in the scores. Students he knew should have scored high in certain areas simply failed to do so. Something was wrong.

As the students began to enter the lab they asked how they had performed. Putting on a cheery face, David replied, "There's been a reporting error. I'm going to have your scores reevaluated." But David knew that a second run of the answer sheets would yield the same results. He just didn't want to tell the students that the Aclare project had failed. He put the test results in his desk drawer and began the day.

David was alone in the lab during lunch when Superintendent Ken Keegan walked in. "David, did you see the test results?"

"Oh, yeah, Ken. I've seen them. I've read them and wept. I don't know what to make of them."

"When the scores came to my office this morning, I looked at Aclare first. I don't understand it, David. Every time I've observed the lab, and that's five or six times over the semester, I knew the students were engaged. I could see it. I could feel it. I've been in education over twenty years. I know what learning looks like, and, by God, the kids in this lab were learning."

"Then why didn't it show on the test scores?"

"David, I don't know why the test scores are so bewildering. I just know the project was a success. I came to see you with hope that you had an explanation that would give me reason to continue the program next year."

"Ken, I only wish I had what you're looking for. Can we ask for another assessment? Could there be a computer malfunction?"

"There's no mulligan on this one, David. It's a cold, hard contract with one shot at performance. We can't cry foul and ask for a reassessment. All the other scores across the school look normal. There were no screwups there. Over the semester Aclare got a lot of attention, not only in this district but in dozens of districts and in the Cities as well."

"Tell me about it. I felt like a tour guide some weeks. We had a lot of observers."

"You did your job, David. As a matter of fact, you did a great job. But in our insanely data-driven mindset, we're told not to trust what we see but only to trust the numbers. In this case, I swear, the kids are getting screwed."

"Then it's done?"

Keegan drew a long breath, pulled a student chair from beneath a cubicle and sat down. "David, you know the pressure that was put on this pilot. You wanted it to succeed, and its detractors wanted it dead on arrival."

"You can say that again."

"The stakes are so high now, not just for St. Luke but for the nation. Public education, at least the public ed world I've known all my life is about to change. It's teetering and when it hits a tipping point, K through twelve in its current form will slowly slip away. Oh, public education will always be around, but today's structure, which I am dedicated to preserve and improve, won't hold. The demographic, economic, and technologic forces are simply too profound, the pressure too great for it to continue as is. The Aclare project gave me a look at what may be, what probably will be, a part of that future. But I won't turn this twelve-hundred kid district into the epicenter of a national soap opera, a drama of public schools against private enterprise. Our students don't deserve that and neither does this town. It's a no-win situation. It's not good guys versus bad guys. After watching this pilot, I tell you, David, private enterprise has no monopoly on greed and public schools no monopoly on virtue."

"Then I'll ask again," David said. "It's done?"

Keegan stood up, "Unless you've got a clear explanation. *The Leader* already has the scores and will run a story in the morning. Once that happens, the whole state will know, and those districts that were interested will turn their attention elsewhere. You won't be able to get the cat back in the bag once these scores are made public. The opponents of Aclare across the country will celebrate and dance on the grave of this pilot program. Yes, something happened here that smells rotten, but we just don't have the time or the system or the money or the people to do a postmortem. We'll just genuflect at the altar of empiricism. I'm sorry, David."

"I'm sorry too," David whispered, as Keegan left the room.

Knowing the program's fate was sealed once *The Leader's* story on the test results appeared in tomorrow's edition, David spoke to the students during the last half hour of the day. The students were shocked. There was total disbelief.

"Mr. Anderson, Aclare works."

"This has been the only good semester I've ever had."

"I know more and think more clearly than ever, thanks to Aclare."

"If I hadn't gotten picked in the lottery, I was going to drop out; now I want to go to college."

"Mr. Anderson, you can't let them close it down."

"We're going to protest."

"We'll stage a walkout."

David appreciated the passion of his students but knew it would dissipate like morning dew.

After school David didn't go straight home; he knew he'd get a call from *The Leader.* Instead he went to a part of St. Luke he rarely visited, his old neighborhood. David hadn't been in the Inkers' Bar since his father had died just days after David's graduation from Iowa. The room grew quiet and everyone stared. He walked to the bar and ordered a Grain Belt. As he was walking to a table, someone yelled, "Thought you were too good to come in here. Your old man's spinnin' in his grave."

Someone else said just as loudly and gruffly, "Shut up, you old fart. Leave him alone. He can drink anywhere he wants."

David was three sips into his beer when Tom Jorgenson, his father's best friend, sat down beside him. "Don't mind that idiot Arne Slater, David. He doesn't have the sense God gave a pickled herring. You here because Aclare got dumped?"

"How'd you know, Mr. Jorgenson?"

"Jim Belson's kid came home with the news, and it spread like wildfire, at least in this part of town."

"Do people in this part of town care about Aclare?"

Tom Jorgenson took a long pull on his beer and pushed his Twins cap back. "You're darn right they care. We were all suspicious last fall when we first heard about it, but that Taylor fellow seems like a straight shooter. The kids from around here who're in Aclare have nothing but good things to say about it. Why do you think the test scores didn't make the grade?"

"I don't know. I don't know."

"Your father would've been proud of you for stickin' your neck out to try to improve things."

"Thank you, Mr. Jorgenson."

"You know, he and I finished high school together and went straight to work for Gram. It's been a good life there. But things have changed. The world's changed. I don't see how Gram can employ another generation of workers. People's backs aren't as valuable as they used to be, but their brains are."

"I know what you mean."

"The money we earn at Gram Industries we spend, and it's gone. But the knowledge you put in kids' heads, that's something you can't exhaust. It keeps growing. More learning equals better earning, and that's what you've been fighting for with Aclare."

\* \* \*

WHEN DAVID GOT HOME, Victor was there. "Ken Keegan called and told me the test results."

"Yeah, he dropped by my classroom as soon as he heard."

Victor passed Anna to Katy. "I pushed Keegan pretty hard on his analysis of why the scores not only failed to show the progress required to keep the contract but also were all over the place, 'pattern-less' was the word he used to describe them."

"What'd he say?"

"Ken had already done his homework by pulling the scores for the last two years of every kid in the pilot and compared their performances. Like I said, Ken called it 'pattern-less.' He confirmed my suspicion when he said he suspected the data had been manipulated. I'm more blunt. I say the results were sabotaged."

"Sabotaged?" David said dumbfounded. "Ken said something had gone wrong, but he never mentioned sabotage." David had never considered the possibility. He had only thought of his own short-comings and questioned whether he had run the program correctly. He sat down, looking as if he had a hundred-pound pack strapped to his shoulders. "But why? "Quickly gathering his senses, he added, "I know the why, but who? Who and how?"

"David, there are plenty of people threatened by Aclare's success. You know as well as I do. And Katy and Ken Keegan and all your students and their parents know. Aclare didn't fail, and you didn't fail your students. Those test scores were sabotaged, changed, manipulated in some form or fashion."

"So if they were sabotaged, and if Ken thinks so too, why won't he try to continue the program?"

"That's a tough question, David," responded Victor with a weary tone. "I asked Ken the same thing. His response was vintage Keegan, clear, sharp, and analytical. He said no, it's not worth it."

"Why not?" David and Katy said in unison.

"Ken thinks we may not need to legally prove that the tests results were sabotaged. In his view the test results are so screwy, just let a couple of good statisticians from the U of M compare the kids' past scores to these, and they'll doubtlessly recommend your students get retested."

"Sounds good. How do we start?"

"Here's where Ken is way ahead of us. He sees the big picture. He'll have to work with the Minnesota Assessment Board to convince them that something nefarious is afoot. That'll take weeks. Then more time to enlist the U to get some professors to examine the data. All the kids will need their parents' approval to allow the professors to examine several years of test scores. Then the profs have to do their work. Weeks more. We're at midsummer at best. Even if they get another chance to test, the kids will be scattered, have jobs, and be in a summertime frame of mind. All of that makes sense in and of itself, but there are two other things to consider. One, the entire schedule for next year has been on hold pending whether Aclare continues or not."

"Yeah, I know, Victor. But we've worked on two different schedules, one if Aclare continues, and one if it doesn't."

"True, but as Ken sees it, there are a lot of personnel decisions, positions to be posted, people to be interviewed and hired. If Aclare's not back, seventy-five kids go back into the mainstream, and with all the retirements and resignations, he's already scrambling for faculty. He's got to staff up for next year under the assumption that Aclare's dead."

David ran his fingers through his hair, "Geez, I thought we had a shot, a shot to reevaluate the program. But what's the other aspect?"

"The politics and the contract. If Ken fights this, the association will bring huge pressure every step of the way for people not to allow Aclare a second bite at the apple. There's nothing in the contract with Aclare that anticipated anything like this. There's no chance to cry foul. No chance to let the kids stay put while the questions are answered."

"Anything else?" David asked, exhausted by the prospect of fighting for months over the test scores.

"Criminal charges."

"What?"

"If the professors make a case that the scores don't reflect the students' abilities and the students retest next fall and do better, as we know they will, then there'll have to be an investigation of what happened. If someone tampered with the test results, there'll be criminal charges. I think this is a very likely scenario. The specter of Aclare will hang over St. Luke for years while this drags on. I want Aclare, but I don't want to bring this community down. I don't want to put St. Luke through that. We have to pick our battles. The time and energy spent on something like that is not only unproductive but counterproductive. We know who wanted this program to fail, and we know how invulnerable they are. A conviction might send some poor louse to prison, but we'll never get to the people who pulled the strings."

There was silence in the room. Ticking clock stillness. A minute passed before David said, "We need to tell Jack."

"I can do that."

"No, Victor, I'll call him."

"Right. It's best you call him." Victor hugged Katy, put his hand on David's shoulder, said he was sorry, and left.

Around nine, David said, "I'd better call Jack and get it over with. You know, Katy, losing St. Luke won't mean anything to Aclare from a financial perspective, but Jack poured himself into this for Victor. Jack's going to be so disappointed. Succeeding in St. Luke had become a personal challenge for him. I think he certainly wanted to show that even small districts are important for Aclare, but I also think he wanted to win this for Victor. There was something very personal in his attention to St. Luke."

Katy squirmed in her chair.

"I wasn't planning to say anything until after the test scores had come in, and Aclare had proven itself to St. Luke, but that's screwed."

"Say what?"

"Well, Jack has asked if I would be interested in joining Aclare, working on improving the program, training teachers, making a difference in the lives of students I'll never meet. He said he'd want me to lead St. Luke for another year before taking a corporate position, but during that year, he'd like you and me to come to San Francisco four or five times for me to work with the development team."

"When did Jack tell you this?"

"Well, it began when I was in D.C., but he'd often bring it up through the winter."

"What did you tell him?"

"I told him I wanted to concentrate on St. Luke. If the test results were as good as we expected, then I'd talk with you, and together we'd decide what's best. With these test results, that option's gone. He'll want nothing to do with me. Jack's the future of American schooling. I've let him down." David walked to the kitchen and picked up the telephone.

"Sit down, David," Katy said softly, "I need to tell you something."

Two hours later, David called Jack. When Jack heard the news of the test scores, he immediately concluded sabotage. There was no emotion in his reaction to David's news, just another piece of business data. There was no talk of retesting or challenging the test scores. No anger against injustices, manipulation, politics over kids, association control over learning. No talk of David's future with Aclare.

Jack asked how Katy was and how she had enjoyed France. David reported that she was fine and had a wonderful trip except for the bicycle accident on her next to last day in France. Jack didn't respond. The conversation lasted less than three minutes. David didn't tell Jack to keep his hands off Katy. He didn't tell him to go to hell. He didn't tell him that he knew he had been used by Jack. He didn't tell him that those in power need to live by the rules. Aclare was dead in St. Luke. Jack Taylor had shaken the dust of the Minnesota farm fields from his Italian leather loafers. He was gone. On to bigger things. An educational drummer selling salvation to a desperate system. An infected doctor spreading a new kind of illness.

Chapter 19

# Second Saturday in May, The Minnesota Fishing Opener

IT HAD BEEN LIGHT FOR OVER AN HOUR when David arrived at Carl and Bobbie's. He parked on the side of the driveway and walked around to the boathouse. The door was open and the lights were on, but as he walked in, he knew something was wrong. Carl's boat was still up in the hoists. It hadn't been readied for a new fishing season. "David? David, is that you?" he heard Carl's voice calling from outside the boathouse. David walked to the lakeside of the boathouse and saw Carl loading gear into his twelve-foot aluminum boat, the one he used mainly to do maintenance on the dock.

"Good morning, Carl. Is everything all right?"

"David, everything's fine," Carl huffed, back turned to David as he arranged the fishing gear, "I'm just running a bit behind and haven't gotten the boat ready for spring yet. I figured we could just go out in the twelve-footer." When Carl turned to slide a tackle box beneath the middle seat, David was stunned. Carl looked like he had aged ten years since the fall. He was stooped, moved slowly, and had drooping bags under his eyes.

"You betcha, Carl. It'll be great to fish the Opener," David said. He bent to put his gear in the boat and thought how glad he was that he had worn two pair of socks and had a hooded sweatshirt underneath his heavy jacket. He was happy to fish with Carl, but he knew he would be a popsicle after three hours in an aluminum boat since the ice had been off the lake for less than two weeks.

Carl climbed to the back of the boat while David pushed them off the dock and hopped into the front. "Where do you think we should try this morning, Carl?"

"Let's go," Carl puffed as his third pull on the motor got it cranking. "Let's go to the drop-off just around Penn Point." He rubbed his side and shoulder as he groused, "For crapsake, if I had my rig out, we'd be there already, but in this tub it'll take us eight or ten minutes."

David turned and faced the bow. He used the roar of the engine as an excuse not to try to carry on a conversation. The air was cold on David's face. The lake was smooth. As the sun strengthened, mist rose from the water. He could see only a few other boats in distant corners of the lake. It was a glorious morning for an Opener. David closed his eyes and enjoyed this ritual of Minnesota, this start of summer, this golden morning, and this chance to mend his relationship with Carl.

It took close to fifteen minutes to reach Penn Point. David was surprised there were no other boats in sight. Lots of people fished at Penn Point where the water stayed five to six feet deep from shore, then dropped off sharply to about twenty-five feet. Carl's fish finder, which was in the other boat, almost always indicated fish along the drop-off. Even without the fish finder, Carl and David knew the best spots for action. Carl cut the engine and let the boat drift on the glassy surface.

In keeping with the quiet of such a peaceful morning, David whispered, "How's Bobbie?"

"Fine, just fine. And Katy and little Anna?"

"Just great. You know Katy went with Sara Jenkins to France with a dozen students last month."

"Oh, yeah, how'd that go?"

"Terrific. They all had a great time," David said, frustrated that he and Carl were speaking to one another like acquaintances, not friends.

Over the next half hour, David tried to initiate conversation with Carl on multiple fronts. He began to wonder if he was trying too hard. Then he chuckled to himself, remembering that silence is a critical component of Minnesotan conversation. But that wasn't it. Carl didn't seem to want to talk to David. In fact, Carl seemed a bit hostile in some of his curt responses.

Silence persisted as the cold crept from the aluminum hull through the soles of his shoes and into David's feet. He was turning into the popsicle he predicted and with no fish biting and no camaraderie, David was ready to try another spot. "Carl, how about we try that spot just off the third hole at Northern Pines? We'll be in the sun and out of the wind if it comes up." David turned to catch Carl's response. Carl was sitting motionless staring at the water. "It won't take us long to get . . ." David stopped talking as Carl, ashen faced, slowly turned toward him. Carl mumbled, "I'm not feeling too well. Can you get us back to the boathouse?"

"Sure, Carl, let's just reel in and head back. They're not biting anyway."

"I don't think . . . I don't think I can . . . I can crank the engine."

"I'll take care of that." David reeled in their lines. "What's wrong, old friend? You look kinda tired. Let's get you back home and into bed," David said. He carefully switched seats with Carl, the little boat tipping one way then the other. Carl didn't speak further. David thought Carl should rest on the floor of the boat between the seats, but that would have been miserably cold. So he sat Carl in the bow seat facing the rear of the boat. That way Carl wouldn't have the wind in his face and David could watch him better.

They were about halfway back to the boathouse when Carl slumped to his left side. A twin outboard was roaring at full throttle, kicking up a significant wake. David turned the twelve-footer to cut across the wake and slowed the engine. "Hold on, Carl, we got a few bumps ahead." The boat cut through the first wave of the wake and was ready for the second when Carl totally collapsed to his left. As his body leaned over the starboard gunwale, the second wave flipped the boat.

David had never felt such intense, muscle-numbing cold. He was heavily clothed and felt for a moment like he was in suspended animation, neither dead nor alive but in between. In ice-cold, clear water with bubbles all around him, his face popped to the surface where he gasped, choked, and comprehended what had happened. Where was Carl? The boat was upside down not ten feet from him, but Carl was nowhere to be seen. Was he on the other side of the boat out of David's sight? Did he surface? Was he alive? Was he alive when he hit the water?

David made his way to the other side of the boat. Carl was not there. He then dove under the capsized vessel. Carl was floating underneath, his head out of the water in the air pocket beneath the boat. He was breathing but not conscious.

David was quickly growing fatigued and numb. When he tried to move Carl, he found Carl was somehow stuck to the boat. He felt down both of Carl's legs and discovered that the left cuff of his pant leg had wrapped around an oar lock keeping him face up under the boat. David untwisted the cuff, wrapped his bad arm under Carl's chin, and pulled him under the capsized boat into the open water. He found a life jacket and slipped it under Carl's right arm for added buoyancy. David looked around. It was about 150 yards to shore. He scanned the lake for another boat but saw only the twin outboard moving away in the distance.

David began backstroking Carl toward shore, his bad arm under Carl's chin and his good arm wrapped in layers of sodden clothes. David swam for two exhausting minutes puffing and blowing in rhythm to his stokes, "Be Thou my vision." Gasp. "Oh, Lord of my heart." Gasp,gasp. "Naught be all else to me." Puff. "Save that Thou art." The numbing water began to overtake his prayer song. He began to recall his beloved American literature and stuck on Nicholas Monsarrat's, *The Cruel Sea*, remembering that sailors in World War II could survive but for a few minutes in the North Atlantic.

He looked over his shoulder. He'd made little progress. He saw the capsized boat thirty yards away and second guessed himself. He should have stayed with the boat. A hundred yards to shore or thirty back to the boat? But he couldn't hold Carl and himself on a capsized twelve-footer. He was near panic, ready to abandon Carl when he heard people yelling and the low rumble of a boat motor approaching.

Closing in on David was Ruth Jordan, the substitute science teacher, and her retired husband. With the Jordans pulling and David trying to push with what little strength remained, they got Carl partially out of the water. David yelled, "Hold him there," and swam to the other side of the boat where a wet nylon rope was his only aid in pulling himself into the boat. David and Mr. Jordan dragged Carl over the gunwale.

Ruth dialed 911 as Mr. Jordan got the boat to top speed. David began cutting Carl's wet clothing away with a pair of scissors from the Jordans' tackle box, ready to wrap Carl in Mr. Jordan's parka, when Carl opened his eyes. "David," he slurred, "David, I'm sorry, so sorry."

"Carl, don't worry about it. We've got plenty of fishing still ahead of us. We'll be on shore in just a few minutes. We'll get you to the hospital and you'll be fine."

"No, David, no. I'm sorry. I screwed Aclare," he slobbered, "I switched the scores sheets. I had to. For Bobbie. For Bobbie. They were killing her, killing her." He closed his eyes. His chest rose and fell, rose and fell in rapid shallow breaths.

"Carl, Carl, don't worry. Just hold on," David cried.

# Chapter 20

# A New Season

Few things of importance came in the mail anymore. The trip to the mailbox at the end of the Andersons' driveway was a daily routine to pick up bills and junk mail. David pulled a stack of envelopes from the box, walked back in the house, put the mail on the kitchen counter, and gingerly rolled on the floor to play with Anna.

It was Saturday, a week after the Opener. Carl, who was still unconscious in St. Cloud Hospital, had suffered a stroke in the boat. Ironically, capsizing had probably worked in Carl's favor. The frigid water had forced his body to keep its blood supply focused on vital organs. But despite that, Carl was on a breathing machine. Attempts to bring him off the machine had not been successful. Earlier that week, David and Katy had visited him in the intensive care unit. A volunteer at the desk told David and Katy she would let Bobbie know they were there. She reported that Bobbie had not left Carl's side.

A minute later Bobbie emerged from the ICU, looking exhausted. With tears in her eyes, she held David's face and said, "Thank you, thank you for saving him." She hugged David and asked him to go sit next to Carl.

As David walked to the ICU, Bobbie turned to Katy. Two awkward seconds passed. Then Katy wrapped Bobbie in her arms. Bobbie broke into deep, intense sobs. She cried so hard she shook Katy. "Oh, Katy, I'm so scared Carl's not getting better. I did this, Katy." She sobbed even harder. "I've been so wrong, and Carl's paying for my mistakes."

"Bobbie, you're exhausted. Things will get better. Carl's getting great medical care. Just get some rest yourself so you can keep up your strength. You didn't cause Carl's stroke."

Katy guided Bobbie to an empty waiting room while Bobbie sobbed, "But I did, I did."

The two women sat side by side on a sofa in the waiting room. Katy had her arm around Bobbie, who was a mere shell of the woman Katy had seen last smashing a bowl of salad on the kitchen floor. Bobbie's depression and insomnia had worn deeply in her face. She had lost considerable weight, alarming Katy when she first hugged her. Now with her arm around her friend, Katy wondered what troubles Bobbie had been going through and why she hadn't been there to help this woman who was so dear to her. Bobbie leaned her head on Katy's shoulder and continued to cry. "I've missed you, Bobbie," she whispered.

Bobbie lifted her head and looked at Katy's tear-filled eyes. "I've been wrong, Katy, and I lost you too."

"Bobbie, you're not making sense."

"No, I'm making sense. When you run from the truth and live with deceit, you build a life on a broken foundation. Try as you might to make up for your lie, the crack in the foundation ruins everything."

"Bobbie, I don't understand."

Bobbie lifted her head off Katy's shoulder, blew her nose, and moved toward the middle of the sofa so she could face Katy. "In 1975 . . . were you even born in 1975? . . . there was a great deal of unrest among Minnesota teachers."

It took Bobbie half an hour to tell Katy her story, how Bruce Barnes had silently blackmailed her, about her depression and insomnia, and Carl's great supportive love. Bobbie said she had put Carl under too great a strain, that her infidelity decades ago had finally caught up with her, and that Carl, who never knew of the affair, was paying the price for it.

Katy listened without comment. The weight visibly lifted off Bobbie as she told the tale. Katy knew she was the place where this secret had come to die.

When she finished telling her story, without asking for or waiting for comment, Bobbie placed her head on Katy's thigh, pulled her feet onto the sofa, and instantly fell asleep. Several minutes later David walked in and saw Katy smoothing Bobbie's hair, weeping. He sat beside them as his red-nosed wife leaned her head to his shoulder. "Oh, David, dear David, hidden sins have a long half life. We never fully know the consequences of our actions."

"What are you talking about?" David asked gently.

"Nothing, honey. Nothing."

\* \* \*

As David played with Anna on the floor, he felt as achy and bruised as he had after a Big Ten game. He was stacking big blocks with Anna when Katy called from the kitchen, "Did you look at today's mail?"

"No, I just laid it on the counter."

"What's the Minnesota Board of Teaching Excellence?"

"Don't know. Why?"

"You got a letter from them."

"I did?" David groaned as he stood up and walked to the kitchen. He uttered a few low "hmms" as he read the letter then, stated flatly, "Well, of all things. Talk about ironies. Katy, I'm Minnesota Teacher of the Year."

"Let me see that," Katy responded with far greater enthusiasm. She grabbed the letter out of David's hands and read quickly, "'. . . chosen from 150 nominees . . . consistent outstanding testimonials and references from people with whom we spoke . . . the finest example of what the children of Minnesota deserve . . . to be honored at a banquet on May twenty-fifth.' David, this is wonderful," Katy said, throwing her arms around him.

"Thanks."

"Thanks. Is that all you can say? How about yippee? Or, this is great?"

"Gee, Katy. I'd forgotten I'd even been nominated. I never thought I'd win. Of course, it's an honor. I guess. It's just so unexpected it hasn't sunk in yet."

"Well, let it sink in. *Vous êstes le meilluer professor du Minnesota.*"

"It sounds nice in French."

"It's an honor in any language."

In bed that evening, David said, "Katy, I don't mean to be unappreciative of being named Teacher of the Year."

"Oh, I don't think you're unappreciative, but you didn't seem very thrilled when you opened the letter."

"Trouble is, honey, I'm not sure I want to go back to the classroom next fall."

"You're usually pretty tired at the end of a school year, David, but you always recharge over the summer."

"I know. But this is different. So much has happened this year. It's changed my views, not on teaching but on schooling. On how we educate our kids. I don't think everything's settled yet in me, but if I had to decide today, I wouldn't go back."

"David, that's perfectly understandable. This year's had more than its share of seismic activity. Winning Teacher of the Year doesn't mean you have to go back to the classroom next fall."

"I guess you're right," David said as he painfully adjusted his position in bed.

"How's your back?"

"Somewhere between sore and miserable."

"Let me rub it for a bit."

"That would be great." David rolled over just as the phone rang.

Katy answered. "Hello . . . Bobbie? Bobbie, is that you? . . . Oh, Bobbie, I'm so sorry. I'll be right there." Katy hung up the phone. "Carl's gone. I'm the first person Bobbie called. She needs me."

"God no," David said, "I thought for sure he'd pull out of this. I just knew he'd make it." He rolled over face down in his pillow.

Katy lay on top of David. After a moment she said, "I have to go to the hospital."

"Shall I bundle up Anna and come with you?"

Katy thought for a moment. "No, let's not disrupt Anna. She needs her sleep, and so do you. I'm really not sure what to expect, but I know Bobbie needs me, and I know I can help her."

David made Katy a thermos of coffee as she dressed and packed an overnight bag. She kissed David at the door and said, "I'll call you as soon as I know anything."

At Mass the next morning, there was an audible gasp from the congregation as Carl's name was read in the petition for prayers for the recently deceased. David got a lump in his throat and held Anna tightly.

After Mass, people lined up to express their condolences to David. He appreciated the kind words about Carl but bristled at accolades of heroism for saving him.

David made his way to the back of the church where several others shook his hand. He looked around for Monsignor Murphy, but didn't see him, and headed for the door. Suddenly the church seemed absolutely quiet, and David realized that he and Anna, asleep on his shoulder, were the only people in St. Ansgar. He turned and went back to sit in the silence. After a few minutes, Monsignor Murphy joined him. "David, I'm so glad you're still here. I was trapped after Mass and uncharacteristically couldn't shake myself loose from a good Catholic," he said with a twinkle in his eye. "How are you? Where's Katy?"

"I'm okay. Sore and sad, but okay. Katy's at the Tuckers'. Bobbie called Katy right after Carl died, so Katy packed a bag and went to St. Cloud. She called just before we came to Mass. She got Bobbie home and was encouraging her to get some sleep."

"This is going to be hard, very hard, for Bobbie. She's not been well for several months." Monsignor shook his head.

"Monsignor, I didn't know that. We've been a bit out of contact with Carl and Bobbie these last months."

Murphy placed his hand on David's shoulder. "I know, David, I know. Your work with Aclare put a great strain on your relationship with them."

"How did you know?"

"It's a small town, David, but more directly, Victor. He's been worried about you and Katy. Does he know about Carl?"

"Yes, I reached him in Korea this morning. He's heading back as quickly as possible."

"I know he's in Korea. He wished he didn't have to make that trip. Gram Industries under foreign ownership. It's hard to imagine."

"Gram Industries owned by anyone but the Grams? That's hard to imagine."

"David, I know you said you're okay, but Carl was very important to you. Along with Victor, he shaped this town. Kept it vibrant. His funeral is not only going to bring St. Luke to a standstill, it'll bring out the entire Minnesotan sports community."

"I hadn't thought of that, Monsignor. I've just been praying for his recovery." David paused. "And now for his soul."

Monsignor Murphy closed his eyes for a moment. "Carl's death is a great loss. Bobbie will struggle. You've lost your friend and mentor. This community has lost one of its most influential and respected people. There'll be a lot of focus and expectation placed on you, and your dramatic rescue of Carl is likely to gain further attention."

"Monsignor, I nearly abandoned Carl out there. If the Jordans hadn't—"

"David," Monsignor cut him off. "What you nearly did doesn't matter. What you *did* matters."

David slowly shook his head back and forth more in confusion than understanding.

"David, listen carefully. In coming days you're going to have considerable pressure on you to step into Carl's role. Don't be swept up in the emotions to take on things you may not want. You have many talents, David, many ways to serve God. Make sure you determine what will have the white hot intensity of your focus."

David was still puzzled. "Monsignor, are you advising me not to take the head coaching job?"

"David, it's much bigger than that. Make sure you use your talents to their fullest. Circumstances have brought you to a crossroads—among Aclare, Carl's death, and Gram Industries, you have many choices. Consider them prayerfully."

"Gram Industries? Victor is in Korea selling the business," David replied.

"We'll see what Victor did when he returns. But you, my lad, have choices ahead—some of your making, some not. Prayerfully consider your next move."

David nodded. He now understood Monsignor's message—listen with the ear of your heart.

Monsignor excused himself as people were beginning to arrive for the next Mass. David sat for another minute and stared at the crucifix. He decided then and there he would tell no one that Carl had switched the answer sheets.

When he got home the phone rang. Expecting to hear Katy's voice, he was surprised by Ken Keegan on the other end. "Hello, David. I want to express my condolences on the passing of Carl. I know how close the two of you were."

"Thank you, Ken. He will be missed."

"I also want to congratulate you for being named Teacher of the Year. I just learned this morning when I came into the office and picked up yesterday's mail. This is a great honor for you and the district. It looks like I missed the official call from the Board of Teaching Excellence while I was out of town on Friday. I had two phone messages from them on my desk."

"Thanks, Ken. I was totally surprised when I got my letter."

"Well, you shouldn't have been. You're an outstanding teacher. Plus, you had the courage to lead Aclare when others were afraid to try something new. It's fitting that you were selected."

"Thanks."

"Between Carl's death and your nomination you have a lot to think about."

"I'm beginning to understand that."

"I just want to express my sorrow on Carl's passing and my happiness for you and St. Luke on being Teacher of the Year. I also want to let you know the district wants you to be a part of St. Luke in whatever capacity you choose."

"Thanks, Ken."

David hung up and quoted aloud from *Julius Caesar*, "Men at some time are masters of their fates."

\* \* \*

KATY MADE IT HOME JUST BEFORE SUPPER. Bobbie had slept most of the day, so Katy had taken calls and received food from people expressing their sympathy and support. Bobbie's older sister, Regina, arrived that afternoon from Fort Worth. Immediately on her arrival, Regina told Katy to call her Gina, "Regina and Roberta have always been Gina and Bobbie."

Together Katy, Bobbie, and Gina spent two hours at Gorby's Funeral Home making arrangements. The few hours of sleep Bobbie had gotten that day barely helped. She was weak, weepy, and indecisive, so Gina and Katy planned Carl's service. After Katy left Gorby's, she came directly home. Gina was more than capable of supporting Bobbie. Katy would step back in once Gina returned to Texas.

The next three days were intense. On Monday, Carl's closed casket sat in the center court of the main gymnasium. From nine in the morning until two o'clock a steady stream of people paid their respects, filing by and touching the casket or kneeling for a moment. Traffic around the school was chaotic. The media was thick. Never had St. Luke been such a center of attention. David was interviewed over and over about the rescue and was constantly asked if he would take over as head coach. His standard response: "I'll consider that after I get over the shock of Carl's passing."

At two o'clock the line of mourners ended, and a school-wide service was held. Ken Keegan; Stewart Tyler, the high school principal;

Reverend Robert Kemmer, Carl and Bobbie's pastor; Monsignor Murphy; Bobbie; and David sat in folding chairs behind the casket. Keegan and Tyler each spoke briefly, powerfully relating a different aspect of Carl and a life lesson for the students. The students listened in rapt silence. Bobbie did not speak but held up well in front of the hundreds of eyes watching her.

When David got up to speak, the student body rose as one and gave him a long standing ovation. David worked to keep his composure. He turned from the students and pulled out his handkerchief. Ken Keegan spoke directly in his ear over the thunderous applause. "This memorial is for Carl. But these kids are cheering you. You saved Carl. You're the Teacher of the Year. You led Aclare. You teach Minnesota writers. You touch their lives. You care."

\* \* \*

DAVID TOOK TUESDAY OFF to be with Bobbie at Gorby's Funeral Home for a family and friends' day of remembering Carl. On Wednesday the district closed for the largest funeral ever held in St. Luke. The Reverend Kemmer and Monsignor Murphy presided. Though Carl was Methodist, the Reverend Kemmer wanted Murphy involved as an indication of Carl's importance to the entire community of St. Luke. The streets were lined with people along the route from the First Methodist Church to the cemetery for the private burial. Many held their St. Luke pompoms, wore their St. Luke sweatshirts, and stood in silent respect as the hearse passed. After the burial, David and Katy helped Gina host relatives at the Tucker house. The Andersons were exhausted.

Moments after getting home, Victor came by. It was the first time they had had a chance to talk with him privately since he had arrived Tuesday morning from Korea. He too was fatigued from the stress of cutting short his business trip in order to hurry home. They sat at the table. Harriet, Victor's cook, had stayed with Anna and reported that Anna had been busy all day and was already bathed and in bed for the evening. After Harriet left, Katy asked Victor how things had gone in Korea.

"Well, Katy and David, I went to Korea to finalize terms for selling the company. Carl's unexpected death provided a legitimate reason to return home and suspend discussions in Korea. My bankers returned to California, and I got here as quickly as possible. Somewhere over the Pacific, I heard a voice that clearly said I had never counseled with you two about the sale of Gram Industries. I think I had always presumed that you, David, would teach and coach and that Katy had little interest in business. Perhaps Carl's passing opened my eyes to seeing things differently. In addition, David, your actions with Aclare took courage and brought out a side of you I had not appreciated."

David shifted in his seat, "Well, Victor—"

Victor proceeded. "No, David, let me say this. The Aclare debacle made me face reality. Even if Aclare had been a success, it was too little, too late. I tried to use my leverage to improve the school district, the opportunities for our graduates, and Gram Industries in the process. But things didn't go that way. My reaction was to call the Korean group that has been after Gram for years and proceed with discussions.

"Not talking to you was wrong. I apologize. Gram Industries is not just mine. It's ours, and I hope that one or both of you will take an active role in being the fourth-generation owner."

Victor stood up. "You both have my sincere condolences on losing such a dear and close friend."

As he headed to the door, Anna began to cry from her crib. "I think I'll go have a good cry myself while rocking Anna back to sleep," Katy said as she headed upstairs.

Victor stopped and turned to face David. He paused, looked down at the floor, exhaustion etching his face. "David, I also must say something else to you man-to-man. This is not the best time, but it's as good as any with Katy upstairs." He looked at David. "You remember the night you kicked Sharon Lunsford out of your hotel room? Well, the bathrobe didn't end up in her room, it ended up in mine."

David leaned back to absorb Victor's revelation.

"Further, you've been operating under the assumption that Sharon resigned her teaching job to take a position Bruce Barnes set up for her. That's true, but I'm still in contact with her."

"What do you mean?"

"When I answered the door and saw Sharon in a bathrobe, it didn't take a genius to know what was happening. I had no idea that you'd just dismissed her, but I knew that she'd been sent to compromise me or, I now assume, you. And whether she did or not was irrelevant. It is much harder to disprove what never happened than to prove what did happen."

"I'm not following you, Victor. Sharon was sent to compromise you and or me. I understand that, but what did she report in St. Paul," David whispered angrily, "that she performed a Gram Slam?"

"David, you're drawing the wrong conclusion," Victor said with some impatience. "I knew what she was there for so I bought her off."

"You what?"

"The truth is meaningless in such a situation. She could easily have reported that she screwed you and me and no one would be the wiser. Who's to know?"

"Funny, that's exactly what Sharon said to me when I refused her."

"What did you reply?"

"I said, 'We would.'"

Victor stood silent for a moment, then said, "My daughter married a better man than I have ever appreciated."

"So, what happened, Victor? What do you mean you bought her off?"

"I didn't care what she reported about me, but I did care about Katy. I told her that if she would leave you alone and that no rumor started regarding the Gram family, I would make a significant

178

contribution to Bruce Barnes' springtime home building extravaganza. The house that will be built next week in Waite Park is a gift from an anonymous donor, yours truly. "

"But, Victor, there was a rumor."

"Yes, but not much of one and it was not started by Sharon. I hadn't anticipated the bill for the bathrobe arriving at the district office. Thank goodness the rumor never got legs. By the grace of God, Melvin stepped right into the middle of it and he doesn't even have the credibility to start a good rumor."

"But how do you know Sharon didn't have a hand in that stillborn rumor?"

"Since that evening in San Francisco, Sharon has kept in contact with me. She works for a small lobbying group in D.C. Barnes is a client of the firm and so is Gram Industries."

"Why are you telling me this, Victor?"

"Because Sharon thinks Carl sabotaged the test scores."

David's stomach lurched. He sat down. "She's crazy. She's out of her mind. Why would Carl have gotten involved? He hates the association and he was about the most apolitical person that ever lived. If you couldn't punt it, hit it, catch it, or shoot it, Carl didn't give a shit about it. Never. I don't know what happened, but I know Carl didn't have a damn thing to do with it."

Victor studied his son-in-law. "I'm sure you're right, David. I probably should have said the same thing to Sharon when she suggested Carl. It's easy to blame those who can't defend themselves."

Victor went out the door. David felt the earth tremble once again.

*       *       *

IT WAS A BLUSTERY, LATE SPRING evening when Katy and David walked into the St. Paul Hotel for the Minnesota Teacher of the Year dinner. In the ballroom, David saw more people than he had anticipated. He quickly counted eight seats per table and estimated fifty tables. He presented his tickets to an attendant, who escorted them to the table directly below the podium. They were the last to arrive at their table and joined Victor, Ken Keegan, Stewart Tyler, Bobbie, who was escorted by Monsignor Murphy, and, of all people, Melvin Vilsak.

David looked around the room. In the corner he saw two tables of his colleagues and people from St. Luke who waved and whistled when they saw him. Sam Tolofson, from the *St. Luke Leader*, was among the press at the event. Several local news stations had their cameras ready.

David and Katy took the last two seats at the table, with Victor on Katy's left and Keegan on David's right. Without being too obvious, David tried to see who else was in attendance. Were there really four hundred people willing to pay to attend the event and give up a Saturday night? He could see several table markers that helped explain the large attendance. Numerous local corporations had purchased tables. David could see signs from his vantage point at a number of tables: Target, General Mills, Famous Dave's, the University of Minnesota, and Gram Industries.

There were five seats on the dais to the side of the podium. David recognized several people, but the name tents before each of them disclosed the strangers' identities. The governor and the Minnesota Secretary of Education were familiar faces, but the name tents revealed the chair of the Selection Committee, the U.S. Department of Education representative to Region 8, and last, Bruce Barnes.

Ken Keegan leaned over to David. "Have you changed your speech?"

"Not one word," David responded as he reached for his glass of water. Two days ago David had dropped off a copy of his acceptance speech as a courtesy to Ken. It wasn't a typical acceptance speech, at least David didn't feel it was, and he didn't want Ken to be caught off guard.

Ken had called David at home with his response. "David, I appreciate you giving me a chance to read your acceptance speech. I don't like it, but I wouldn't change a word."

During dinner the governor stepped down from the dais and shook hands with David, Katy, Victor, and Ken. He apologized to David that he had to leave to attend another dinner. A few moments later, Minnesota's Secretary of Education and Bruce Barnes stepped down to congratulate David. After shaking hands with David, Barnes went around the table to Bobbie. He hugged her, kissed her on the cheek, and expressed his condolences on her loss of Carl. Barnes returned to the dais, leaving wreckage in his wake.

Katy tapped David's arm after Barnes left. "Hey, didn't the governor just tell you he had to leave early?"

"Yeah, why?"

"Because he was supposed to introduce you."

David looked at the program. "Oh, well, he probably sloughed off that auspicious duty to his Secretary of Ed."

As dessert was being served, the chairwoman of the Selection Committee began the recognition ceremony. Three teachers were presented with Honorable Mentions, one elementary, one middle, and one high school teacher. Each was brought to the podium for a plaque, handshakes, and a photo.

David looked at the program. It was time for his introduction and speech. With his right hand, he felt inside his suit coat for his speech while Katy squeezed his left hand underneath the table.

The ballroom quieted as the chairwoman nodded to Bruce Barnes. Barnes went to the podium. "The governor called me several days ago when he realized he had a conflict this evening and had to attend two events. He asked me to apologize for his having to leave early and asked if I would do the honor of introducing Minnesota's Teacher of the Year."

David grinned at the irony. He looked at Bobbie, who was stone-faced, staring at the candle flame in the center of the table.

Barnes's introduction was accurate, personal, and jovial. He made David a Minnesota icon—a St. Luke native, a football hero, an outstanding coach, a loved teacher. He praised David's courage for leading Aclare, for "not being afraid to try new ideas to benefit the students of our state."

Ken leaned over and spoke in David's ear, "Try not to barf on that bastard when you get up there." When Barnes relayed David's rescue of Carl, Bobbie's eyes poured. Katy switched seats with her father to be next to Bobbie as David took the podium to a standing ovation. He was presented a crystal apple on a walnut base and a framed proclamation signed by the governor. After three quick photographs, he stepped up to the microphone.

"Thank you. It's an honor, and one I never expected, to be named Minnesota Teacher of the Year." He looked down at the table below him and saw people he loved. For a moment he felt light-headed, almost in suspended animation, like when the boat capsized. He took a sip of water, mentally tightened his chin strap, and paused for a moment to look around the room, to appreciate the moment. He was ready.

"In accepting this honor tonight, I was asked to speak about my career and the importance of education in Minnesota. I am a proud product of Minnesota public education. My mother died when I was twelve, and my father worked at Gram Industries in St. Luke. My father was a quiet man who dedicated himself to seeing me through college. Even though I got a scholarship to play football, I think my dad kept himself alive until I graduated. Then he let himself go, his work on earth finished. May his soul and that of my mother rest in peace." David heard a scattering of "Amens" across the room.

"As I noted, I played football in college. As such, I prepared for a teaching career that I would take up after pro football. An injury, a life-saving injury, ended my playing days my senior year." He looked at Katy through the lights.

"From college I returned to my hometown to an ideal existence. Married to a woman I adore. Coaching with the legend who had coached me. Teaching students in a school where learning mattered, in a community where good manners were stressed.

"Things went along beautifully for years. My wife and I added a lovely daughter to our home, and my teaching grew in depth and breadth. Our football team dominated its opposition. I was a lucky man, moving day to day through a life I had the good fortune to appreciate."

David stopped and looked again across the audience, folded his speech lengthwise and tucked it back inside his suit coat. He cleared his throat, hesitated, and began again. Not from his notes, from his heart.

"This past September I began another idyllic year." He stumbled a bit searching for what he truly wanted to say. "Another idyllic year, not knowing how dramatic it would be, how much it would change me.

"In the fall, the community of St. Luke agreed to let Aclare Learning operate a pilot program on a trial performance basis. Improve the students' performance and the program stays; fail to improve performance and it's gone. A clean and simple benchmark, a true perform-or-perish pilot.

"I volunteered to be trained in the Aclare method and to lead the learning lab for the spring semester trial period." He breathed deeply. "Never before had I seen students so engaged, critical thinking growing, analysis deepening, intellects expanding, students too busy learning to misbehave, students too excited by learning to goof off. It was evident to me that the results of this spring's Minnesota Academic Assessment Test would show growth beyond our greatest hopes. But, alas, the test scores failed to show the necessary growth, and the project ended.

"Disappointed by the failure of the Aclare project, I consoled myself by looking forward to getting back to teaching my fall elective course, Minnesota Writers—Sinclair Lewis, Jon Hassler, Patricia Hampfl, Garrison Keillor. Sadly, I learned in early May that the course would be dropped because it was not aligned to the National High School Assessment.

"Then, my dear friend and mentor, Carl Tucker, had a stroke while we were fishing the Opener. Like so many in our profession, I became a teacher because my teachers had such a positive impact on me. Carl Tucker was the most influential person in my upbringing.

"I am grateful to Carl for so many things: his guidance, his friendship, his knowledge of the game of football, his fishing acumen, his common sense, his role model as a devoted husband. Carl Tucker was a good man, a simple man, not complex, not worldly. His loves and interests were few but deep and complete." Bobbie sniffled. David could see Katy's arm around her friend.

"There was an important lesson Carl taught me this past fall that stunned me by its obviousness and added to the maturation that this school year brought. My wife, Katy, and I were having dinner at the Tuckers' home. It was one of the happiest routines in our lives—dinner with the Tuckers on Monday nights while Carl and I prepared for our next opponent.

"After dinner Carl was grousing about all the attention the community of St. Luke was devoting to the Aclare debate. In his direct and simple way, Carl let it be known that the Aclare debate was counterproductive, taking attention away from the football team. He said that sports—football first, basketball second—is the glue that holds public education together. Sports unite the community. Without sports, support for public education would wither. Sports is the elephant in the room of education reform. Sports dominates our school culture, our identity, our schedules, and our academics." The ballroom was silent as David paused.

"As one who grew up in a culture of sports, excelled in that culture, and then perpetuated it in my coaching, I was stunned by that insight. Please don't get me wrong. I love sports. I love coaching. But Carl's statement was the beginning of an epiphany that has led me to treat sports in a more healthy perspective and to resist the obsessive nature it has in our culture.

"When I told Carl I would have to miss the final game of the regular season and the playoffs in order to be trained for Aclare, he was angry, and there was a breach in our long and wonderful relationship. For me, Carl's reaction to my interest in training for the Aclare project was a microcosm of how our schools respond to change—with anger and fear.

"In my work with Aclare, I found a method of teaching and learning that is truly remarkable and effective, despite what the test scores said. I worked with seventy-five students in one class for the entire day with no problems. And I saw this same program work just as well in blighted inner-city schools in Washington, D.C., Aclare works. It's so successful it threatens the status quo, the way things are today, the stakeholders who have their share of the pie and place their stability and power over the needs and opportunities of the students for whom they are responsible and to whom they are accountable. It's a true tragedy and a genuine travesty that the test scores failed to reflect the academic and intellectual progress that occurred inside the Aclare lab this past spring semester.

"I became a teacher to be a coach. I became a coach to be a teacher. I became a teacher to give to the next generation what I was given, to nurture youth to the greatest extent possible." He had found his stride and could see the finish line. "But I realized this fall that we give to the next generation only from our surplus, from our excess. We don't give them what they need, or deserve, or what is possible if it requires change, or sacrifice, or a loss of power or money from those in charge.

"Our nation was built on sacrifice, self-denial by one generation for the benefit of the next. That national characteristic has run into a brick wall of self-indulgence, self-delusion, and self-absorption. As a result, we have psychopathic schools that dominate children's lives but teach them the wrong lessons. We pour 500 billion dollars a year into public schools but have a forty percent drop-out rate. We lock children in a twelve-year march with others their own age and stifle the joy of children interacting and learning with students of other ages. We place them in a factory model of schooling and wonder why so many never finish the process, why so many of those who do finish come out substandard.

"Schools give students what remains after the adults have taken what they want. We truly fear remaking schools. Too much of our economy is tied to the current structure; teachers, professors, certification boards, textbook companies, materials suppliers, construction firms, bus drivers, cooks, janitors, and counselors all need the current structure, the current money machine. Parents need the current structure, the seven hours a day of state-provided child care so the parents can work to avoid every other state-offered service—housing, food, transportation, medicine.

"It's a crazy position public schooling holds in our nation devoted to individual freedom. The state decides what children are to learn and delivers the teaching with government employees. We used to call that brainwashing. Now we call it standards setting. I believe the founders of this nation, dedicated to liberty long before the advent of public schooling, would look aghast at our education system and fear for its capacity to sustain a free and powerful nation.

"I am honored to be Minnesota's Teacher of the Year. I accept the recognition on behalf of the thousands of excellent teachers in our state who ply their craft and devote their professional lives to children inside a broken, politicized, dysfunctional, and ineffective system.

"Reality hit me just a few weeks ago when my Minnesota Writers course was dropped from the curriculum. Teachers no longer lead students in learning and self-discovery; teachers prepare students for tests. One of the great tragedies of American education today is that politicians run our schools, not teachers, not those close to the needs of the students, but rather those who know little about schooling and are angry, embarrassed, and misguided about test scores.

"America, the lighthouse of the world, champion of the downtrodden, educator of the handicapped, desegregator of society, eraser of gender bias, leader of research, genius of innovation, giant of the arts. America, a nation to which millions yearn to come, is worried that other countries might surpass its greatness. The world should be so fortunate.

"When you have a *Road to Damascus* experience, it is impossible to stay as you were. The experience demands change and a move forward into uncertainty. A start of a new season. That is what happened to me.

This was the last year of the old season. Next September, for the first time since I was five years old, I won't be going back to school."

David stepped back from the podium. A polite round of applause filled the ballroom.

\* \* \*

THE SKY OVER MINNESOTA WAS ELECTRIC. It was almost nine, and the setting sun painted the Andersons' world a shade of fiery rose. They had driven for almost twenty minutes, both holding a secret about the Tuckers, when David broke the peaceful silence. "Katy, I've never looked ahead on a calendar without start and stop dates. I don't know what the future holds. I won't be teaching and I don't want to lead Gram Industries."

Katy reached over and held David's right hand. "Well, I can tell you that the future holds good things for us: love, laughter, faith, friends, Anna, and another baby due right around Christmas."

David slowed the car and eased onto the shoulder of the interstate. He pulled Katy into his arms and whispered in her ear, "*Tres bon.*"

# Acknowledgments

If authors didn't have others, books would never be written. I am grateful to my wife, children, and extended family members for their patience and encouragement; to my friends who read and critiqued; and for the assistance of my agent and editor.